What Others Are Saying

With appeal to all ages, Sebastian's Tale is a story that will fascinate everyone who can peel away the layers and begin their own journey into enlightenment.

WALTER M. BRASCH, PH.D., author of *Fracking America, Before the First Snow*, and other books.

* * *

What I loved most is the possibility (and perhaps reality) of interspecies cooperation. We humans underestimate the potential for working with Nature instead of against it.

IONA CONNER, Founder and Publisher, *The Go-Back Club, A Simple-Living Brigade*.

* * *

Dylan's inventiveness, verbal puns, and fast-moving plot keep Sebastian's Tale exciting and entertaining. This fable is rich in sensory detail and replete with laugh-out-loud humor, melancholy, and fear.

MARAT MOORE, retired editor of the ASHA Leader and author of *Women in the Mines*.

* * *

Sebastian's Tale is an imaginative, thoroughly entertaining story of the quest for enlightenment. Deftly woven into the story are difficult issues like dementia, environmental degradation, and even bullying.

KAREN FERIDUN, Environmentalist and Founder, Berks Gas Truth

* * *

Weiss explores the moral problems and implications of fossil fuel development as land predators threaten the woods in which animals have their home. The book begs readers to evaluate their worldview and relationship with nature.

TARA M ZRINSKI, Author/Illustrator

Sebastian's Tale

A Skunk Tales Trilogy Book

Dylan Weiss

Red Engine Press
Pittsburgh, PA

Library of Congress Cataloging-in-Publication Data

Names: Weiss, Dylan, 1944- author.
Title: Sebastian's tale : a Skunk tales trilogy book / Dylan Weiss.
Description: Pittsburgh, PA : Red Engine Press, [2016] | Summary: "Best friends Sebastian the skunk and Willie the weasel embark on an exciting adventure as they struggle to unravel an ancient prophecy and end a family curse. They must join forces with their friends and neighbors to fight the battle against the destruction of their forest home and its inhabitants"-- Provided by publisher.
Identifiers: LCCN 2016039740 | ISBN 9781943267163 (alk. paper)
Subjects: | CYAC: Skunks--Fiction. | Weasels--Fiction. | Forest animals--Fiction. | Environmental protection--Fiction. | Blessing and cursing--Fiction.
Classification: LCC PZ7.1.W4348 Se 2016 | DDC [Fic]--dc23

LC record available at https://lccn.loc.gov/2016039740

Cover: MaryJayne Reibsome and Joyce Faulkner

Edited by Betsy Beard

Printed in the United States.

Red Engine Press

Dedication

Sebastian's Tale is dedicated to my most treasured and beloved grandchildren: Joey and his sister Dylan, Samantha and her brother Jordan. May they learn the wisdom of the Three R's: Respect, Responsibility, and Resolution. May they have the freedom to forge their own paths and follow them to successful conclusions. May their childhood be one of Pretendment and discovery into adulthood. And may they continue the story of life after reaching Enlightenment.

Acknowledgments

The multiple themes in this fantasy are rooted in my childhood, so first thanks go to my parents, Albert and Marguerite Kronheim, for giving me the positive encouragement all children deserve as they learn to find themselves. Dad fostered my curiosity about and respect for the Earth, and it was Mom who instilled in me a penchant toward activism.

The biggest thank you goes to my grandson Joey, whose early fear of my husband's Alzheimer's became the catalyst for writing *Sebastian's Tale*. Over the eight years it took to complete it, the story became a complex allegory taking on multiple meanings, themes, and messages. None of this would have happened without Marat Moore and Michelle Bourgeois, both of whom deserve huge thanks not only for inspiring me but for their continued encouragement and editorial advice.

Thank you to my sons, Douglas and Mark, who were early readers and critics, along with my daughters-in-law, Shelly and Amy, both of whom are strong, creative women. Thank you to my two sisters, Laura Kramer and Jane Kronheim for their inspiration and encouragement. And thank you to my cherished friend and confidant, Jim Giammaria.

Others who deserve thanks are Dr. Joan Glickstein who introduced me to the joys of writing and speaking, Dr. Kunal Mankodiya who introduced me to the world of social media, as well as Dr. Walter Brasch, all of whom had faith in my project and assisted me in the process of self-publishing.

Part 1

PRETENDMENT

"A single event can awaken within us a stranger totally unknown to us. To live is to be slowly born."

Antoine de Saint-Exupery

~ 1 ~

Number One Is Born and Named

He was the first of three to be born during an early spring snowstorm, not too long before the rainy season, around the end of March. The night was long and the winds were fierce, howling through barren trees. Although the parents tried to protect their offspring, even the comfort they provided by their bodily heat could not warm the newborns from the blanket of icy snow covering Penn's Wood. By morning there was much sadness as Numbers Two and Three were blessed and buried. Number One was the sole survivor and, as his parents were soon to discover, had the misfortune of having been born with a rare genetic defect that set him apart from his family and became the focus of his existence.

Although the parents were both heartbroken over the loss of Numbers Two and Three, it was the mother who felt the greater pain.

"Oh my most respected mate, I am grief stricken," cried Sylvia. "We waited so long and now we have only a singleton."

Sol comforted Sylvia, gently wiping the tears from her face. "Please, my sweet, let's be grateful for this one. He'll make up for Numbers Two and Three. And as Number One, he already is our one and only."

"I know. It's just that right now I'm so very tired. Perhaps after a rest, I'll feel more positive." Sylvia's eyes started to close.

Sol tried to comfort her. "Come dear, it's been a traumatic night. Get some rest while I try to keep our little guy warm and safe.

While Sylvia slept, Sol hovered over Number One. He knew they should perform the initial inspection together, but Sol couldn't wait. So bending down, Sol took a closer look.

"Let's see here ... correct number of feet, a top, a bottom, but where are those familiar family birthmarks?"

Sol fluffed the fuzz on Number One's back looking for the all important insignia and camouflage critical to their family's existence. However, they weren't there! In shock, Sol began to tremble. He gasped and then produced a frightening, bloodcurdling squeal and shouted, "Sylvia! Sylvia, wake up! There's something very wrong."

Sylvia opened one eye and looked at Sol. "What? Sol, let me be, I'm so tired."

"No, you must awaken," Sol insisted.

"Why?"

"Because you need to check. I think our little one has a defect."

Sylvia struggled to wake up. "Defect? What kind of defect?"

Panic stricken, Sol answered, "Our family birthmarks. I can't find them."

"Oh Sol, I'm sure the marks are there. They must be."

"Please, Sylvia, just get up and have a look for yourself."

Sylvia's inspection of Number One began in a gentle manner using her eyes. When she didn't find what she expected, her apprehension grew. Nervously she began brushing the top fuzz with a forceful back and forth movement as she searched and prayed. Number One squirmed.

"Sylvia, stop being so rough. Can't you see you're disturbing him? Now...are you satisfied? See what I mean? They just aren't there!"

There was a long significant pause before Sylvia answered. "Oh Sol, I'm so very sorry. I thought nothing like this would ever happen. I've ... I've been keeping it a secret."

"Secret? What secret? What do you mean?"

Sylvia sighed. "I have something to tell you, and it's a long story."

"About what?"

"It's about my Great[1], Great[2], Great[3], Great[4], Great[5] et cetera Grandfather, the one who is known to all as the Greatest Grandfather to the Fifteenth Power of Greats."

"Sylvia, do you mean to tell me you can trace your family roots all the way back to ancient times?"

"Yes, Sol, that's exactly what I mean." Sylvia sniffled.

Sol already knew the story since it was the cornerstone on which Enlightenment School was founded. "Sylvia, please stop crying. I think I know where this discussion is leading, but I'm not ready to hear the truth. Tell me after we eat. It's been several days and I'm hungry. You must be hungry, too. And our little one needs to eat. I'll get some food while you take care of Number One and collect your thoughts."

Sylvia used her right paw to wipe her nose and dry her tears. Then, fixing her eyes on a distant point on the opposite wall, she contemplated how best to explain.

Sol left his family in the den and darted up to the entrance of their home. Poking his nose out and sniffing the chilly air, he knew that foraging for food wouldn't be much fun. At least, not until the middle of the warm season, when his favorite berries were fat and juicy. He gathered an evening meal of grubs and bugs, all the while pondering the consequences of raising a flawed offspring. Then he hastened back to the den, where he and Sylvia ate in silence, both thinking of the talk they would soon have. After finishing their meal and checking to be certain their little one was safe, protected by newborn slumber, Sylvia and Sol retreated to a different part of their burrow to talk about Sylvia's ancestry and the fate that had befallen their kit.

Sol faced Sylvia, giving her an encouraging smile. "Sylvia, my Sylvia, as beautiful as our woodlands, why didn't you tell me that you're descended from the most famous of all skunks in skunkdom, the one who discovered skunk stink?" Sol's smile grew bigger. "That Captain Norton Bulymur is your Great Grandfather to the Fifteenth Power of Greats?"

"Because I was afraid," Sylvia whispered.

Sol scratched his head in puzzlement. "But, what were you afraid of?"

"First, I was afraid that you might select me as your mate only because I come from a famous family. Second, I was afraid that you might not select me because of the stripeless gene I carry that could someday afflict one of our kits. And now it has. Number One has no stripes." Sylvia buried her face in her paws.

Wrapping his arms around Sylvia, Sol said, "None of that matters to me. We'll get through this together. Now that we have Number One, we're a family. And there's no turning back."

Sylvia hugged Sol in relief. "Thank the stars you are so understanding. You can't imagine the anguish I've had, keeping this secret from you. We'll need to provide Number One with extra protection because of his deformity."

Sol shook his head. "Sylvia, we can't over protect him. If your Great[15] Grandfather was able to overcome this adversity, then so must our kit."

"You're right, but—"

"Sylvia, no buts. Now let's name our little kit. We can't call him Number One forever."

Sylvia nodded. "Okay. Let me think about names. I was named after the vast forests of Penn's Wood, and you were named after the sun. How perfect that we have given each other a new life, a kit born of the woods and the sun. We need to bestow upon Number One a name reflective of the challenges that await him."

"Obviously, he should be named after your Great[15] Grandfather, Captain Norton Bulymur. After all, it was Norton who was the first to be born without stripes and thus the one in which the genetic curse began. So let's name our kit Norton."

"I think Norton is old fashioned. How about if we use the first initial of Norton's last name, a B-name for Bulymur?"

"Sylvia, I think you're right. Perhaps a B-name is a good idea. How about Bud?"

"Too short. How about Bartholomew? I kind of like that."

"Too long. Sylvia, what do you think of Bastian? It's short for Sebastian, Patron Saint of Soldiers."

Sylvia squealed in delight. "Oh, I love the full name Sebastian ... Sebastian Mephitidae."

"Who knows, Sylvia? Maybe our Sebastian will grow into his name. You never know. Someday he may indeed become a soldier." Sol puffed out his chest in pride at the thought.

So that's how Number One, the only surviving kit of Sol and Sylvia, became known as Sebastian.

~ 2 ~

Willie the Weasel

Mephitidae are home-schooled from birth through the first year of life, a time known as the Year of Pretendment, when all is carefree with uninhibited discovery, often mischievous in nature. As such, Sebastian's parents encouraged him to play make-believe, at least until the beginning of his second year, the Year of Enlightenment. Thus, he remained in the family den under the watchful eyes of his parents who fed and cared for him, and taught him the basics about being a skunk.

But neither Sol nor Sylvia mentioned anything about skunks having stripes. And they never told Sebastian about his stripelessness. Instead, wanting him to feel special for a different reason, they focused on Sebastian's thick, glossy coat of fur.

There was one very important thing Sol and Sylvia told Sebastian, and that was about his cousin Willie, a weasel, who lived quite a distance away near the Deep Creek. Despite the distance, the parents kept in touch.

In the forests, it was always a small mouse that was entrusted to deliver messages, going from wood to wood and family to family. This method of communicating was known as m-mail. Sylvia had just received a disturbing message from Willie's mother Wanda and was reading it to Sol in hushed tones, as she didn't want to disturb Sebastian, who appeared to be asleep.

"Oh no, Sol, this is terrible," Sylvia said as she read the note delivered earlier in the evening.

"What, Sylvia? What's wrong?"

"It seems Willie's first few weeks attending Enlightenment School did not go well. According to Wanda, Willie is being bullied by the other kits because of his large size. Now he hates going to school." Sylvia looked up from the note and glanced over to where Sebastian lay sleeping, an expression of concern on her face.

Sebastian, both blessed and cursed with curiosity, often feigned sleep when he wanted to gather information. And so, on this occasion, like so many others, Sebastian heard every word of his parents' conversation.

Sol silently followed Sylvia's eyes, his thoughts on Sebastian's future and worried that his stripelessness would keep him from being accepted by his peers. Sebastian, still pretending to sleep, wondered why one kit would be mean to another. He just did not understand meanness.

As Enlightenment approached, it would be time for Sylvia and Sol to prepare Sebastian for the next phase of his development. His stripelessness would need to be explained.

10

Little did they know that life would soon take a sudden turn, and the explanation would come from a surprising new addition to the family.

* * *

Like Sebastian, Willie was named after his own Great Grandfather to the Fifteenth Power of Greats. In the olden days, Willie's Great[15] Grandfather, Mordecai Wilhelm, an eccentric inventor, had been best friends with Sebastian's Great[15] Grandfather. However, unlike his namesake and other weasels that were generally long and thin, Willie was short and fat.

Willie's troubles began shortly after he entered Enlightenment School. His parents, Wanda and Webster, suspected he was being teased by classmates at school. He was hesitant about leaving the burrow, and each day when he arrived home, he was breathless and his whiskers twitched nervously.

About a week after he started school, Wanda asked, "What's wrong, Willie? Every day you come home looking upset."

Instead of responding, Willie hurried past, heading for the pantry for a snack. After eating his heart out by filling his stomach, Willie broke down and told his mother about the relentless ridicule from his classmates. There was one ferocious fellow in particular, Wolvie, who was half weasel and half wolverine.

Wolvie had learned from his dad how to control his peers. Daily, he would strut through the school-yard, puffed up with arrogance and anger, which he consistently directed toward Willie.

"There goes Wide Willie," Wolvie sneered, his voice raised to be heard.

A group of about ten other classmates, known as Wolvie's Pack, chimed in lest they, in turn, become the brunt of Wolvie's internal rage which was flipped inside out. The Pack's unified voice echoed the taunt until it became a chant. "Wide Willie, Wide Willie, Wide Willie."

If that wasn't dreadful enough, it got worse when Wolvie made up a contest called Weigh Willie. The Pack attacked Willie in the gym locker room shoving and pushing him onto the scale. That's when the guessing began. The weasel coming closest to Willie's weight was the winner.

"You know what the prize was, Mom? It was getting to chase me home after school." Willie shuddered.

"No wonder you hate going to school. Is this what they call Enlightenment? No one should be treated that way, especially not you, my wonderful, precious son." Then she licked his wounds.

"Mom, puhleeease," said Willie, pulling away. "Whatever you do, don't tell Dad. He'll insist on going to the headmaster, and that'll just make things worse."

So nothing changed for Willie until a few days after the talk with his mother. A day that otherwise would have been ordinary suddenly became extraordinary, forever upsetting the balance of nature in the woodlands of the Deep Creek.

A series of loud menacing blasts sent Willie racing from his after-school explorations of the forest's perimeter back to his family burrow. Willie recognized the sounds, since he had already witnessed the same booms and devastation in differing parts of the forest. The cause of the noise was a new and hungry enemy, land predators who gulped down trees, wildflowers, and animal homes without hesitation.

As he ran home, debris rained down. Willie tried to duck, but he was temporarily knocked out when one of the flying rocks hit his head. As he came to, Willie felt dizzy, and there was dried blood on his head, but he staggered on. Despite what was happening, he was able to find the place he once called home.

To Willie's horror, all had been pulverized by a hoard of giant monsters. They looked like metal soldiers dressed in uniforms of varying colors, some red, others yellow, green, or orange. Some had one or two eyes made out of glass that glowed in the dark, and they smoked, exhaling a smelly substance that suffocated the wildflowers and killed some of the smaller animals.

Suddenly, Willie heard muffled cries from the mound of rubble and debris that was once his home.

"Mom, Dad ... is that you?" With his sharp claws, he dug furiously at the ground.

Willie didn't need to dig far before Webster surfaced and shortly thereafter, Wanda, who moaned as she pushed her head through the dirt. Their fur was as dull and dusty as ancient relics.

"Thank heavens you found us, son, or we would have been buried alive," Webster said with relief. "Mom's right paw is badly crushed, and you have a heck of a lump on your head. We need to get to Dr. Patchup, pronto."

Together, Webster and Willie pulled Wanda out of the devastation. The three escaped from the rubble and slowly made their way to the doctor, with Willie carrying Wanda on his wide back.

Dr. Patchup examined Wanda. "I'll bandage your paw, but it won't ever be the same. Even after it heals, it'll be a source of pain. As for you, Willie, you're a brave one. That lump on your head may cause you some difficulty in the future."

Dr. Patchup waved as the weasel family turned to leave, knowing then that his home was also in peril. Like the rest of his weasel relatives, he had mistakenly thought they would remain safe in their part of the forest forever. Where would they all go? It was such madness.

Webster's thoughts echoed Dr. Patchup's. "Dear ones, we need a new place to live, but with all the excavation going on, it'll be impossible to replace our burrow. We'll need to downsize."

So the family moved under a rock farther from the construction site. It was an uncomfortably tight squeeze, with little room for a still growing Willie. After much deliberation, Wanda and Webster decided the best solution was for Willie to live with cousins Sylvia and Sol, who maintained a large burrow in one of the forests of Penn's Wood. Wanda sent a brief m-mail to Sylvia.

Burrow destroyed, sending Willie to live with you. Please meet us at the Breezy Wood in three nights.

Wanda and Webster accompanied Willie as far as the Breezy Wood, where a tearful delivery was

made. Sylvia, Sol, Wanda, and Webster hadn't seen
each other in a long while, but there was no time
for an extended visit. The kits were busy talking
and getting to know one another when Willie's folks
indicated it was time for them to leave.

"We'll m-mail at least once a week and visit
often, so don't worry. You'll be fine," Wanda said
with tears in her eyes.

After hugs, Wanda and Webster turned away and
began trudging back to the Deep Creek. With dismay, Willie watched as his parents, tails swishing
simultaneously like the pendulums of side-by-side
clocks, grew smaller and smaller, until they seemed
to be nothing more than a couple of dots disappearing in the distance.

* * *

Sylvia and Sol were delighted to have a friend for
Sebastian. He and his cousin Willie soon became like
brothers. Understanding their need for private space,
Sol built them a treehouse from a small felled log
which was rotting behind their burrow. It was close
to a clear stream, and one could hear the peaceful
gurgling of water washing over rocks and pebbles.

The treehouse became a hideout where the cousins spent countless hours. One day, during a discussion about their differences, Sebastian learned
about his stripelessness.

"Ya know Sebastian, back in the Deep Creek
when I went to Enlightenment School, I got to see
skunk kits, and you look different."

"Different? Whadya mean, look different how?"

"You're missing something."

Sebastian shook his head in confusion "What am I missing?"

"Well, all the skunk kits I met had white stripes just like your Mom and Dad. And you don't," Willie pointed out.

"Ya mean I'm not just like Mom and Dad?"

"No, like I said, you're different. We're both different. Not just different from each other, but different from other skunks and weasels. I'm supposed to be long and thin but instead, I'm short and fat. And, you ... well, you're stripeless."

"Is that a bad thing?" Sebastian wondered.

"Considering my experience during the short time I went to Enlightenment School, being different isn't a good thing. The other weasel kits were mean, teasing me about being fat."

"Willie, that's terrible. What about me? Do you think the skunk kits will tease me for not having stripes?"

Willie rolled his eyes before answering. "Uh ... probably."

For the first time in his short life, Sebastian felt a surge of anxiety.

"But Mom says my fur is thick and beautiful, so why do I even need stripes?"

Willie shrugged, "I don't know, except all the other skunks have them, so they must be really important."

"Why are they important? What are they for?"

"I think they're some kind of protection."

"Protection from what?"

"Don't know that yet."

"I'll ask Dad what they're for."

"No, don't do that. They must not want you to know, at least not yet."

"Maybe they're waiting to see if the stripes to grow in?" Sebastian asked.

"Maybe, but I think by now they would be running down your topside from nose to tail tip." Willie gestured to Sebastian's tail.

Sebastian turned his head, trying to see down his back. "If they don't grow in before we go to Enlightenment School, can you help me find some?"

"Sure, and you can help me lose weight."

Willie and Sebastian shook paws to seal the deal.

The next two weeks the kits spent endless hours in their tree house as Sebastian created weight loss plans for Willie, and Willie thought of ways to help Sebastian get those all-important stripes.

* * *

"Now Sebastian, you know that your Year of Pretendment is almost over, and Enlightenment School begins midsummer." Sylvia stated, patting Sebastian's head.

"I know, Mom, but I'm scared. Do I have to go?"

"I'm afraid so. It's hard for me, too. I wish you could stay with us forever, but we need to follow the Rules of Skunkdom. Dad's waiting for you in the study. He has something he wants to discuss."

Sylvia gave Sebastian a gentle nudge in the direction of the study, then went back to her sewing room where she was creating a present for Sebastian. It was a special backpack made out of black canvas, with two bright white stripes running down the outer section. She had designed it herself, hoping it would disguise Sebastian's stripeless defect. Sylvia felt uneasy as she sat, sewing away and pondering the fate of her kit with this obvious deformity.

Sebastian entered Sol's study where he found his Dad shuffling papers strewn on top of the desk. "Dad, you and Mom can teach me everything I need to know. I don't really have to go to Enlightenment School."

Sol shook his head. "I know, I know. I felt the same way when I was your age, but it's necessary. You must learn how to forage for food; scent an enemy from a distance; and interpret messages from the ground, sky, and trees as well as from other animals. Most importantly you will learn how and when to use your skunk stink. Sebastian, you know that Pretendment is the time for make-believe and imagination, frisk and frolic, trial and error. However, during Enlightenment, the learning process is formalized and you will be schooled in the Three R's."

Sebastian asked, "Whadya mean, the three R's? What's that?"

"You'll find out soon enough. All I can explain is that it's the code of honor to which all skunks and other kits belonging to our larger family must adhere," Sol replied solemnly.

"Dad, is that all? Are you done with your talk?"

Sol became uncomfortable and his speech hesitant. "Um, well, uh ... Sebastian, there are a couple of other things you need to know about the Year of Enlightenment."

"What is it, Dad? And why are you acting so weird?"

"I am not acting weird."

"Yes, you are. You're scrunching up your face like you always do when you're nervous."

"Sebastian, you're being rude and that's unacceptable."

"Sorry, Dad. Okay, what is it?"

"Well, Son, during this special year all the animals in the Mephitidae family are transformed from childhood into full-fledged adults."

Then Sol blurted out, "That means you find a mate, a new place to live, and make skunk babies."

"Oh that? I already know about that. Cousin Willie told me. No biggie!"

Much to Sebastian's surprise, Sol, whose fur had become matted with a musky perspiration, seemed greatly relieved instead of becoming angry.

"Can I go now? I'm supposed to meet Willie. We have plans."

"What plans?"

"Dad, I already told you. Plans."

Willie was waiting for Sebastian behind the burrow in their treehouse.

"Willie, you won't believe what just happened. Mom told me to have a talk with Dad in his study. I thought it would be about my absent stripes. Know what he wanted to tell me? All about how after Pretendment ends, we need to find our own places to live, take mates, and make kits. He was so nervous he was sweating. So I told him I already knew all about it from you."

"Why did you tell him that? Now he'll be mad at me for talking too much."

"No he won't. He really seemed relieved."

"Did you say I also told you about being stripe-less?"

"No, I didn't ... I promise."

"Okay, then. Let's get out of here. We're wasting time and I feel restless." Willie's whiskers were twitching as he anticipated adventure.

~ 3 ~

The Newton Neighbors

It was summer and the solstice was only a few weeks away. After playing all night with Willie at the helm, the kits wandered into a clearing miles away from their home. As the morning sun bathed the clearing with warm light, Sebastian and Willie cautiously approached the backyard of a people house. Both knew they had stayed out all night and should have headed for home long ago, but were too curious to turn back.

At the edge of the yard Sebastian and Willie stood motionless, adjusting to the smells, sights, and sounds of this new world. They could hear the trickle of water that gently spilled down the sloped back yard, pooling into a small pond near the brick patio next to the house where a new and different sweet smell lingered in the breeze.

The land sloped steeply downward with many trees which stretched southerly in their attempt to catch the sun, creating a tipsy look to the backyard. There were many gardens surrounded by paths dappled in sunshine and shade.

Sebastian, nose to ground, examined the growth about the yard. "What are those green plants with the big ears?" he asked Willie.

"They're called hostages."

"Why? Were they captured or something?"

"Could be," Willie answered. "Maybe because their ears grew so big, they might of overheard some private conversations. So they were taken hostage. Now they're stuck under that tree with their ears in the ground forever."

"Well, that makes sense," Sebastian said, scanning the yard.

The garden had a variety of colorful flowers, organized in designs and grouped among differing sized rocks.

"What are those called?" asked Sebastian, for he had never before seen flowers like the garden varieties.

"Flowers mostly have lady names like Petunia, Daisy, Violet, Iris, and Rose."

"Why do they have lady names?"

Willie was proud to be mentoring his younger cousin, but really didn't know the answer. He paused and after giving it some thought, said, "Well Sebastian, ladies use perfume to smell pretty, and flowers also smell sweet. I think that's the reason most flowers have lady names."

Willie was puffed up with his own self-importance for having imparted this logic to Sebastian.

"Are there man flowers, too?" asked Sebastian.

"Well, I see a Tom-ato plant over there. That's a man flower, because it starts with a man name.

Sebastian answered with a simple, "Oh."

To maintain his influence, Willie continued schooling Sebastian regarding flowers. "As you noticed earlier, these flowers are different from the wildflowers that grow on our forest floor. So if they're not wild, they must be tame. And therefore we don't need to be afraid of them."

Sebastian still looked worried, his gaze drawn to the snapdragons that Willie had also pointed out. The two continued meandering through the gardens, and then Willie noticed something he had never seen in the dark woods before.

"Sebastian, look! See there in front of me? It's a flat, grey shape, and it's attached to my paws. When I walk it follows me, and it's long and thin. Maybe I could become it, and then the weasel kits at Enlightenment School won't tease me. What do you think it could be?"

"I don't know, but I have one, too. Maybe all the other skunk kits have the same attachments. If that's so, then their stripes won't show up, and we'll all be the same."

They continued exploring and pondered the consequences of their attachments.

As they scanned the yard, Sebastian and Willie were attracted to the clothes hung on a clothesline. They headed toward the line, running quickly through the snapping dragons that, after all, were most hospitable. Getting closer, they could see that the line was made of rope. To Sebastian and Willie, the rope appeared to have pinned down prisoners. When the wind blew, the captive pants, shirts, socks, and one gray-green jacket, flapped and jerked, attempting to escape.

"Look over there, Sebastian. The jacket and one of the shirts just made a getaway and are on the ground. Come on. Let's see if we can help 'em."

Sebastian and Willie crept closer to the line with its escaping garments. They were now near enough to discern the letters "A.N." on the grounded pink shirt. Sebastian stood frozen, eyes fixed not on the monogrammed shirt, but rather on something else.

"Look! Look there, at the jacket. It has stripes!"

What the two didn't know was that the backyard was Newton family property. The pink monogrammed shirt belonged to Abigail, the owner of the house, and the faded old jacket, with its stripes affixed to each shoulder sleeve, had belonged to Abigail's dad, the late Albert Amster, who was a celebrated World War II hero. His mothball preserved jacket was being aired out to wear for dress-up by Abigail's grandson, Simon, who was visiting for a few days.

Sebastian's eyes grew misty with a faraway expression, "Oh, Willie, how I wish those stripes were mine. They are so beautiful. If I had them, I would be like the other skunks."

"Come on, Sebastian. I'll help you. I bet I can get 'em off with my claws."

Just as Willie was closing in on the jacket, the patio door of the house slid open. A golden-haired boy of about six came running out, a cookie clutched in one hand and a football in the other. "Mimi, some animals are sniffing around Papa Al's army jacket," the boy yelled.

A buxom lady with short dark hair and a pleasant face bolted through the door, wiping her hands on a white apron. A large barking dog named Oliver followed Abigail out the door as she ran after her grandson.

"Simon, don't touch. Leave the animals alone," she ordered while waving her hands about. "Shoo! Shoo!"

When the dog spotted the woodland animals, the chase began. With Willie in the lead, the two kits ran in a zigzag manner, confusing their pursuer, who finally lost interest once the pair crossed into the woods.

~ 4 ~

The Dawning of the Age

It was well into the next day before Sebastian and Willie got back to their den. Just before reaching its entrance, they stopped to catch their breath. Between gasps, they carried on a raspy conversation.

"Listen, Willie, we're in deep trouble now. You realize we pulled an all-dayer. Mom probably started having one of her famous worry fits! We're doomed."

Willie, in a cool manner although also out of breath, said, "Oh Sebastian, you worry too much. She'll be so relieved to see us that her anger will simply disappear. We'll end up with hugs, kisses, and hot cocoa. Just act calm."

Dirty, worn, and tired, they slipped into the den, hoping not to awaken Sylvia or Sol.

Sylvia, standing upright with her upper paws crossed against her chest, right hind paw tapping, and whiskers trembling in agitation, waited just inside the den entrance. Her face, usually bright and welcoming, was stern, and the kits knew they were in trouble.

"Okay, you two. I can just imagine where you've been. Look at you, you're a mess. And you know what's coming."

"Oh no, stop! Not a bath," each chimed as Sylvia bathed the kits, scrubbing them hard and mercilessly.

"This should teach you not to stay out until after daybreak. You deserve exactly what I'm giving you," Sylvia said as she applied the dreaded smelly antiseptic shampoo.

Sebastian and Willie yelped, "Oooh, ow! That stings!"

Sylvia liberally lathered a special tree sap into their ratty fur, all the while giving them a good tongue lashing. However, at the end of it all, as predicted by Willie, Sylvia gave them a cup of cocoa along with forehead kisses, before tucking them into bed for the remainder of the day. Willie gave an I-told-you-so glance to Sebastian.

After Sebastian and Willie were fast asleep, Sylvia sought out Sol, who was in his study reading the headlines of the *Tree Tribune*. He was hunched over, giving a ruffled appearance to the stripes down his back. As he read, Sol sipped a cold bitter brew that Sylvia prepared from her humulus plant. She made it using an old family recipe which she had received along with a cutting from her mother, who had received it from her mother, who had received it from her mother, going all the way back to the beginning of skunk time.

Sylvia gently stroked the fur on Sol's back while recounting the kits' misadventure and expressing her fears that mischief would continue between the two. Then she added, "My honored mate, Sebastian is growing up quickly and will soon leave his Year of Pretendment, and since Willie will repeat the first two weeks of his formal schooling, both will enter Enlightenment School together. The summer solstice is almost here, and it's time they learn about their ancestral history."

"Yup, so it is. And this isn't just an ordinary solstice. Indeed, this one may prove to be magical. Last night, while studying the stars through my telescope, I saw Jupiter align with Mars."

With a telling expression on his face and a sly smile, Sol continued, "Sylvia, my love, do you know what that means?"

Sylvia was exhilarated. "Sol, are you positive?"

"Yes, m'dear, there it was ... big old Jupiter smack dab in front of Mars!"

Ecstatic and breathless with excitement, Sylvia said, "Sol, finally! It's what skunks across the world have been waiting eons for, the dawning of the Age of Aquarius. If the predictions come true, 'peace will guide the planets, and love will guide the stars'."

Sylvia clasped her paws, looked heavenward, and continued her rapture. "Do you remember what our sages prophesied? It's predicted that during the Age of Aquarius the curse of the stripeless coats will have an opportunity to be lifted. The time has come. We must begin the ceremonial reading of our family history, *Die Alten Tage*. The kits must learn about the adventures of their Great Grandfathers to the Fifteenth Power of Greats."

Sol glanced up at Sylvia, and thoughtfully stroked his whiskers.

"Those two shared notorious times, didn't they? Clearly the kits are drawn to each other in the 'now-adays' the same way that Norton and Mordecai were in the 'olden days.' Like their ancestral counterparts, Sebastian and Willie are inseparable. Sylvia, I agree with you. We must hasten the reading, for I sense that we'll be unable to change the course of fate."

~ 5 ~

The Sacred Bundle

In the beginning, the stories were an oral history, passed on to every skunk and weasel during their Year of Enlightenment. Eventually the tales were written down by a Skweasel Scribe, a rare breed within the family and conceived in an uncommon union between a skunk and a weasel. Mother G, as she was referred to, penned the furry-tales in a by-gone tongue known as Skweadish. The ancient text was buried along with two other relics, together known as the Sacred Bundle. Now it would need to be unearthed from its hiding place.

The day before the intended excavation, Sylvia couldn't sleep. Although she had not seen the Sacred Bundle since her own introduction into Enlighten-ment, she knew its secret location. Sylvia's parents had given her explicit instructions not to dig it up until she was ready to bequeath it to her firstborn upon the initiation of his or her Enlightenment.

At home Sylvia hovered over the kits with antic-ipation. Sol, a security guard at the dam building enterprises of Beaver Brothers Unlimited, was at work physically, but not mentally. He requested an early departure from owners, Bud and Boyd. They met in the conference room.

"Whatsamadder?" Bud, the older of the two beaver brothers asked Sol with concern.

"W-well, you see," Sol stuttered, "Sylvia is the direct descendant of Captain Norton Bulymur and entrusted keeper of the Sacred Bundle, which includes the ancient book that must be read to Sebastian and Willie before the beginning of their Year of Enlightenment."

"No kidding. Djeetjet? Yous wanna eat widdus before ya go?" They spoke with a dialect common to all beavers that lived and worked along the rivers in the western part of Penn's Wood. While some among the skunks had difficulty understanding the beavers, Sol had become accustomed to their speech and had no trouble communicating.

"No thanks, maybe another time. I'm too nervous to eat."

"Hey, we understands. Ya' gotsta do what ya' gotsta do."

Sylvia was preparing the evening meal when Sol arrived home. It was sundown, but the kits were still asleep. Sol, stooped and bleary-eyed, entered the burrow.

"Oh Sol, you poor dear. You look so weary. Why not take a nap before we eat?"

Sylvia went about her duties, while Sol retired to his study. He rubbed his tired eyes and nodded off into a deep sleep, during which he experienced a very strange dream. He was running through an ancient forest, a fugitive without stripes, when suddenly he felt a shocking chill run down his back like a current in a frigid stream. All the while a screeching horned owl chased after him—

Sylvia, who heard Sol yelling, rushed to his side and shook him out of the nightmare. He awoke feverish and agitated. In a shaky voice, Sol told Sylvia about the dream.

"Love, what do you think it means?" Sol asked.

Sylvia looked perplexed. After giving it some thought she said, "Well, perhaps this event really happened in a past life, or maybe it's just a reaction to the events that are now unfolding."

After Sol regained his composure, he and Sylvia formulated a plan to pass on the legends to Sebastian and Willie.

"Sol, I would be honored if you act as Master of Ceremonies revealing the contents of the Sacred Bundle while I translate the ancient text."

Sylvia summoned the kits for their evening meal. During the meal, Sol and Sylvia barely spoke, but the kits didn't notice the tension at the table. They chattered endlessly about their most recent adventure at the wood's edge, where they had again visited the Newton property, despite the dog.

"Hey, Willie, did you notice the man in the back yard talking to the squirrels?"

"Yeah, his name's DJ, and I think he's Abigail's mate."

"What makes you think that?"

"I heard Abigail calling, 'DJ, DJ, where are you?' When she found him wandering in the backyard, she ran over and gave him a hug. But he didn't seem to care, hardly even looked at her. His face looked blank, like a lake without any ripples. He ignored Abigail and mumbled something about the squirrels."

"Did you hear what he was saying?"

"Yeah, he was calling them bad. He kept on saying 'bad squirrels, bad squirrels'."

Sebastian asked, "Why bad?"

"I think because the squirrels were eating the bird food from the feeder."

"Do you think there's something the matter with DJ?"

After some thought Willie said, "I don't know, but he does seem odd. He keeps calling the dog, 'I love her' instead of Oliver."

"Hmmm, that does sound strange."

Sebastian and Willie continued chattering throughout the meal, after which they asked to be excused from the table.

While they were off for yet another night of adventure, Sylvia and Sol dashed to the back of their burrow. An eerie glow created by the light of the full moon beckoned them forward. Carefully they crept out of the small opening toward the hiding place. On the ground, next to a large felled tree, was a fat log riddled with knot holes.

"Sol, it's under here. Ready? One, two, three..."

Sylvia began digging away at the third knot hole to the left of center until it split open, revealing a hollow within. The hallowed hollow was covered over with dry leaves and twigs. And there, buried beneath the thatch and under a blanket of rich dark peat moss, was the Sacred Bundle.

Sol was awestruck. Before him lay an ancient text encased in a thick, brown animal hide. It was held together by a frayed, worn cord wound tightly around the stem of a petrified acorn. Carefully, he untied the twine with its acorn. With a flourish, he placed the acorn around Sylvia's neck and tied the string as he would a precious necklace. "For you, m'dear."

Next Sol retrieved the last item in the Sacred Bundle. The strange stick was gnarled and prickly, radiating a peculiar pulsating glow. When Sol lifted it, the white stripes on his back stood up on end, electrified. He became transfixed, and as he explained to Sylvia, "It felt like my stripes were levitating. I felt cold and bare, just like in my dream."

Sylvia, who understood the powerful magic of the Embla Stick, quickly removed it from Sol's frozen grasp. Only a direct descendant of Captain Norton Bulymur had the ability to guide the Embla Stick. When Sylvia put her paws around the stick, it instantly went from crooked to straight. Its tip began to flicker and flash, making a crackling sound like a sparkler.

With the spine-chilling event over, Sol continued assisting Sylvia with the excavation. He used a whisker broom to brush peat moss from the volume, running his paws over its embossed golden lettering before giving the rare manuscript to Sylvia.

~ 6 ~

The Revelation

Several yester-nights later, the family gathered around the dining table. Sol spoke first.

"Ahem, kits." With a few more throat clearings, he said, "As you can see, there is a very old and very special book in the center of the table. In it are the legends about your Great Grandfathers to the Fifteenth Power of Greats."

The kits looked puzzled and said, "Legends, Great[15] Grandfathers?"

Sylvia picked up where Sol left off, "The stories reveal their adventures, discoveries, and inventions.

"Adventures? Discoveries? Inventions?"

Then Sol continued, "You will learn about their valiant flight from the primeval forests of their beloved Westphalia, how they escaped, and how they brought all the different kinds of skunks in our family to the Americas."

Again the kits interrupted, "Valiant flight ... primeval forests ... escape?"

Then Sylvia chimed in, "Enlightenment is upon you and it's time to learn about your heritage."

Sebastian and Willie together said, "Heritage?" Wide-eyed and full of curiosity, the kits were captivated.

With his right forepaw held high in the air, and his eyes looking up to the heavens, Sol said, "Kits, you must listen carefully, for this year holds the possibility of great change for all of skunkdom. The Age of Aquarius has finally begun, bringing with it an opportunity for a select stripeless skunk to end the family curse."

Taking the words out of Sol's mouth, Sylvia added, "Assuring that all future skunk generations will be born with stripes."

Sebastian couldn't believe what he was hearing. His parents had never before mentioned the family curse which was his inheritance. And now they were telling him about an opportunity to eradicate the curse forever.

Sol reclaimed the floor. "You are now old enough to go into the world, fight your individual battles, and as a result become stronger with the winning. And win you will, if you use the power of the Three Rs."

"Hey!" Sebastian poked Willie. "Dad mentioned the Three Rs to me before, when I was in his study. It's some kind of code of honor."

Sol scolded and then hushed the two kits.

Sebastian and Willie stared silently at Sylvia and Sol. There was a hush in the room as the kits watched Sol again place the acorn around Sylvia's neck.

The thick silence lingered until Sebastian spoke, a trail of questions tumbling out of his mouth.

"But, how will we follow the Three Rs? How are we supposed to know what to do? Why now? Where do we go from here? Will we ever see you again? Who will help us?"

Sol's single but repetitive answer, "Wait a while, wait a while," encompassed a lifetime of experience which seemed to hold some degree of promise.

Sylvia turned to Sebastian and Willie explaining, "Kits, the Three R's, like an invisible shield, will guide and protect you. They include the R of Respect, the R of Responsibility and the R of Resolution."

Sylvia took a deep breath before continuing. "After the reading is complete and the celebration meal over, you must leave this den and learn to forage for yourselves. Sebastian, you are the next in lineage to pass down our skunk heritage. Thus the keeping of the artifacts next falls on your tail. You must respect the artifacts, display responsibility, and be resolute in achieving your goals."

Feeling left out, Willie, asked, "What about me? How do I fit into the picture?"

"Willie, while the Three R's are integral to skunk tradition, the code is also taught during Enlightenment to the weasels and all members of the Mephitidae family. But there is also a special secret that only weasels must learn," Sol answered.

"There is?" Willie asked in bewilderment.

"Long ago the secret was handed down to your Great[15] Grandfather by a friendly fox, one who had heard it from the fox who told a little prince. As you are my adopted son, I have the pleasure and obligation to pass it on to you. You will undergo a transformation when winter comes. It is then that you will come to understand this secret."

Sol paused, his speech soft and slow as he continued, quoting a passage from *The Little Prince:* "One sees clearly only with the heart. Anything essential is invisible to the eyes."

He repeated the passage to make sure Willie fully understood. "One sees clearly only with the heart. Anything essential is invisible to the eyes."

Then Sylvia spoke to Willie. "My beloved son, you must support and guide Sebastian during your respective struggles to find your true natures."

"I understand. I'll always help Sebastian. He's my very best friend and ... and ... brother. But Mom, I'm starting to feel hungry. When do we get to eat?" Willie asked, rubbing his stomach.

Sol explained to both kits, "We will postpone our meal, as it is important to fast and ready ourselves for the opening ceremony. Tonight we need to be hungry for knowledge rather than food."

Willie was chagrined but his hunger was replaced with curiosity.

Sylvia readied herself by closing her eyes and then made a series of beckoning motions with both paws, as if she were ushering in space, time, or perhaps the wind. There was a hush in the den. Slowly, Sylvia turned around three times, all the while humming an old folk tune. It struck a chord of familiarity with Sebastian, who had been rocked to sleep as a wee one by its charming melody. Placing her forepaws on top of *Die Alten Tage*, Sylvia took several deep breaths before clearing her throat and reciting the mystical poem over the ancient text.

May the wisdom of the elders,
Be with me now.
As I read these ancient stories,
I make this vow.
To translate the historic words
On these pages,
Exactly as it was written
By the sages.
I will begin these furry-tales
In a Grimm way,
Starting with Once Upon a Time
Is what I'll say.
And Happily Ever After
Will end all tears,
Replaced with joy and happiness,
Laughter and cheers.

Her recitation complete, Sylvia opened the ancient book. A cloud of dust was released, setting her into a coughing spell. Truth be told, the dust was enchanted, giving all in the room a protective coating. After the dust settled, and the first page revealed, Sebastian and Willie could see that it was written in a strange language. Sol explained that the ancient language, a combination of Skunk and Weasel dialects from the old country of Westphalia, was called Skweadish. The words, engraved on the first of the yellowed parchment pages, looked like this:

Es war einmal, Eine lange, lange, lange Zeit vor, in der Urwald Gesamtstrukturen es lebte Familien Skunks und Weasels. Eine spezielle Skunk, Norton Bulymur und eine spezielle

*Weasel, Mordecai Wilhelm waren das beste
der besten Freunde sowie der Cousins wird.
Armen Norton hatte ohne Streifen geboren
wurde und Mordecai versuchte immer, ihm
einen Weg zur Bewältigung seiner Unterschied
finden zu helfen.*

The kits pointed at the strange writing in the
ancient text and excitedly began whispering to one
another. Suddenly they were brought to attention by
a jagged shard of lightning illuminating the burrow,
followed by the sound of rolling thunder echoing in
the hills. Sylvia picked up the now glowing Embla
Stick and used it as a pointer, touching the right corner of the first page. An astonishing thing happened.

The words were lifted off the page as Sylvia drew
the Embla Stick skywards. One by one, each word
rose up, up, up, into the air, leaving the page below
completely blank. Whirling round and round, faster
and faster, like the twirl of a tornado, the words
finally came to an abrupt halt, suspended in the
air. Then, with a puff of smoke, the twirl of words
tumbled back onto the page. Willie and Sebastian
gasped in wonderment as Sylvia read:

*Once Upon A Time, a long, long time ago, in
the primeval forests, there lived families of
skunks and weasels. One special skunk, Norton
Bulymur, and one special weasel, Mordecai
Wilhelm, were the best of very best friends, as
well as being cousins. Poor Norton had been
born without stripes, and Mordecai Wilhelm
was always trying to help him find a way to
deal with his difference.*

So it was that as the Embla Stick touched the top right corner of each page, the letters rearranged themselves from Skweadish to English, and Sylvia was able to read the furry-tales to the kits.

Part 2

ENLIGHTENMENT

"... Humankind has not woven the web of life,
We are but one thread within it.
Whatever we do to the web,
We do to ourselves.
All things are bound together.
All things connect."

Chief Seattle

~ 7 ~

The End of Pretendment

By the time Sylvia read the last line and proclaimed "The End," it was late the next day. Sebastian and Willie were fast asleep when Embla crackled, sputtered, and pulsed a blue hue as if taking her last breath. Drained of all energy, Embla returned to her former self, the gnarled Skweasel Stick that was part of the Sacred Bundle. Sol gently removed the acorn necklace from around Sylvia's neck.

There was a hush in the room as Sylvia carefully closed the great volume, and ceremoniously bound the ancient text with the thin twine and acorn that she had worn as a necklace, carefully placing the petrified acorn on top. Accompanied by Sol, she returned the Sacred Bundle to its resting place.

Then the two divided up, Sylvia going to the kitchen and Sol going back to check on the sleeping kits, still in the dining-room. Lifting each up by the scruff of his neck, Sol carried Sebastian and Willie, one at a time, to their sleeping space and then joined Sylvia in the kitchen.

"The kits have been mesmerized by the grandeur of the stories and are now in a deep slumber," Sol reported.

"Good. This is as it should be. They need rest before the dinner celebration and difficult farewells. While the kits are in dreamland, I'll prepare the buffet and you invite the relatives to share in the inevitable. Go now and gather the skunk and weasel families. After all have arrived, we will have a full lunar feast."

While Sylvia busied herself in the kitchen, Sol set out to assemble the relatives. As for Sebastian and Willie, they slept soundly with visions of sea captains and first mates, sails and spiders, owls and beavers, and naturally, romance and triumph.

The kits awoke at dusk, rubbed their eyes, yawned, and then turned to one another.

"Sebastian, I had the strangest ..."

Before Willie could finish his sentence, Sebastian chimed in and together they said, "Dreams." Then, catching the drift of special scents floating from the kitchen, they scurried from their sleeping space into the dining room and were astounded to find a long table spread with all manner of foods. The local skunk and weasel families shouted, "Surprise!"

Sebastian and Willie were speechless. Gazing around the den, they spotted relatives, some familiar, others not. Finally their growling stomachs, like personal dinner bells, announced that for them it was time to eat. Sebastian eyed sparrow delight, honeyed bugs, blue robin eggs, and carrot-squash strata, while Willie's focus was diverted to the punch

bowl filled with bug juice and decorated with floating crunchy beetles. Their mouths watered.

"Wow! This is so awesome!"

Sebastian began to dig in and Willie dashed to
the punch bowl.

After the meal was over and compliments to the
cook given in all manners (or lack thereof) of belch-
ing, burping, and "excuse me's," Sol became solemn,
addressing the kits and guests.

"Dear family, we are gathered tonight to say
farewell to Sebastian and Willie, who have ended
their Year of Pretendment. As happens to all skunk
and weasel kits, they must now leave home to enter
their Year of Enlightenment."

Turning his full attention toward Sebastian and
Willie, Sol said, "Kits, we are going to sorely miss
you, but now it's critical that you find a new home."

Sebastian, although Sol had tried to prepare him,
was nevertheless dumbfounded. "I know we need to
leave, but where will we live?"

Willie, too, was dumbfounded. "Who will make
our meals?" he asked, rubbing his stomach.

The kits were visibly shaken. It was Sylvia who
spoke next. "Follow your instincts, for they will
provide you with all the answers."

Sylvia turned her back, went over to a far corner
of the burrow, and retrieved gifts she had stashed
away for the kits. "Now for your special going away
presents. To you, Sebastian ..."

With great pride Sylvia presented the backpack
she had lovingly created. "Son, this backpack will
bring you good luck. You should wear it always, and
never take it off. Here, let's have a look."

Sylvia slipped the backpack over Sebastian's shoulders.

"Wow Sebastian, now you look like the other skunks," Willie said.

"Thanks for the compliment, Willie." Sebastian was overcome. "Gee Mom, I finally have my stripes."

"Not really, Sebastian. These are only temporary. Listen carefully; I need to remind you and Willie of something very important."

"What is it, Mom?"

"Don't forget it's now the dawning of the Age of Aquarius."

"Oh yeah, you mentioned that before. Can you tell us more?"

"Aquarius is a special time. A time we skunks have been anticipating for at least as far back as your Great Grandfathers to the Fifteenth Power of Greats. Not only is it a time of peace and love, but it's also during this Age that the genetic curse of the stripeless skunk can be lifted."

"But, how?"

"The prophecy states that a skunk born of no stripes will earn them through performing good deeds. When that happens, from that day forward all skunks are guaranteed to be born with stripes. Sebastian, since I am a direct descendant of Captain Norton Bulymur, the honor of removing this curse may be yours."

Willie interrupted, "You mean Sebastian can grow real stripes?"

"The possibility exists, Willie. However, they must be earned."

"But how, Mom?" Sebastian asked. "I'll do anything!"

"Sebastian, I don't know the specifics, but as you are schooled in the Three R's, the way will be revealed."

Turning her attention to Willie, Sylvia continued the presentations. "Willie, for you we found a beautiful pearl comb for your winter white fur, which will grow in at the appropriate time." Sylvia looked directly into Willie's eyes, and reinforced his earlier lesson to see with his heart.

After the gifts were distributed and final goodbyes said, Sebastian and Willie left the burrow, but not without great uncertainty.

"Willie, where do you think we should go?"

"Well, Mom said to follow our instincts, and mine tell me to head toward the house with the dog and the old man. At least we know the way and there's always plenty of food in their garbage cans."

"True, but where will we live?"

"I dunno. I'll figure out something. I always do. So let's get going and see what we find when we get there."

Sebastian and Willie scampered through the night until they were again at the wooded perimeter where the forest ended and the people houses began. They stopped, out of breath, and scanned the yard, not sure what to do next.

Willie, never one to be patient if food was nearby, said, "Come on. I see trash cans. And they're full of something. It sure does smell good. Let's check it out."

Sebastian reluctantly followed Willie down the hill through the night-shrouded gardens until they were directly in front of three trash cans. Willie, out of control with excitement, jumped on top of the first one. A loud clanking reverberated into the night's stillness as the lid rolled down the driveway, until it arrived at the bottom, spinning round and round like a top before clattering to a halt.

The sound of the lid was followed by the loud barking of the dog, Oliver. Willie, whose snout was well into the trash can, paid little attention as light streamed from an upper story window.

"Come on, Willie. Let's get out of here or that dog will come after us again."

"Ummm, yummm," was Willie's only response, along with the sound of slurping.

The dog continued barking and Sebastian noted that another light went on, this time in one of the first floor windows. Within minutes a new noise could be heard, that of a distant siren growing closer and louder.

"Hey, Willie, get out of that can. There's some kind of contraption with a blue flashing bar on top. It just stopped at the bottom of the people house driveway."

Two burly police officers walked up the driveway in the direction of the trash cans. It was only then that Willie scampered down from the can, which he knocked over with a loud clang.

"Quick, Willie, run fast!" Sebastian yelled as he ran.

But Willie was too large to keep up with Sebastian, and the distance between them grew. They were scurrying across the lawn in the direction of the woods when Sebastian abruptly disappeared.

Willie slowed and began sniffing the ground. "Sebastian, where are you?"

"Down here."

Willie heard Sebastian's voice coming from beneath the ground a few feet in front of him. He began sniffing around the hole from which Sebastian's voice seemed to be coming.

"Hey, Willie, wiggle yourself in. There's more room down here than you can possibly imagine. Even more than we had back home."

Willie tried to suck in his stomach to make himself smaller, but no matter how much he wiggled, wriggled, and squirmed, he couldn't squeeze through the hole.

"I can't get in, Sebastian. The hole isn't big enough."

"Well then, start digging and make it bigger."

Willie dug around the perimeter and managed to enlarge the opening just enough to jiggle in. "Wow, you really scared me when you disappeared like that."

"Sorry, Willie, it happened by accident. I was running toward the woods when I tripped over the entrance and fell in. Look around. This burrow is huge, and it branches out in all directions."

Once Willie's eyes adjusted to the dim underground space, he saw that it was quite sizable, with offshoots going in a variety of directions. The complex was a series of tunnels, one connected to another, stretching underground across the backyard expanse of the Newton property. The air had the same earthy smell they had become accustomed to in their previous burrow.

"Sebastian, I think this could be our new home."

"Maybe. But what if it belongs to some other animal?"

"Oh, you worry too much! Even if there are other animals, they probably have more than enough room for the two of us."

"I dunno. If other animals live here, how do you know they'll like us? What if they're enemies? Then what? I think it's best if we leave when the dog stops barking and go somewhere else."

"Like where, Sebastian? This is the only part of the woods we know about. I say we climb out, see what's going on, and then come back down here. Let's snoop around before giving up on this place."

When the dog settled down, Sebastian and Willie crawled out of the newly discovered burrow, perked their ears, and listened. Without the barking, the night was quiet enough to hear the conversation between Abigail and the policemen.

"Officers, thanks for coming so promptly. Especially since you were just here the other day helping me locate DJ when he wandered off. The noise woke me, and I really didn't know what else to do at this late hour."

"No problem, Mrs. Newton. That's what we're here for. We're more than happy to check in. How's Mr. Newton doing?"

"Not well. He just started a new medicine, though, so maybe it'll help."

"Good luck. We hope it gives you both some relief."

52

Sebastian had heard every word of the conversation. "Willie, did you hear that?"

"What?"

"About the man they called Mr. Newton."

"I guess I wasn't paying attention. Sorry, I sniffed the food that spilled out of the trash can. It smelled so good I got distracted."

"Willie, you need to pay attention. You know how odd the man called DJ seems to be?"

"Yeah."

"Well, one of the men asked the lady about a Mr. Newton. I think that's who DJ must be. DJ is Mr. Newton and the lady said something about him being not so good."

"I wonder what's wrong."

"I don't know but they're still talking. Maybe we'll learn more..."

"In the meantime, Mrs. Newton, we think your intruder was just a hungry animal attracted to the garbage cans. Probably a raccoon. We're getting a lot more of these kinds of calls."

"Well, I'm not surprised. The poor animals are being driven away from the woodlands by developers that keep building unnecessary homes."

"If you think that's a problem, just wait until you hear what's coming next."

"What do you mean? What's coming?"

"You'll be reading about it soon enough, what with all these companies drilling for gas around these parts. Listen, it's time we get back to the station. Don't hesitate to call again if you have any more trouble."

"Okay, thanks again for all your help."

Abigail sighed as she returned to the house, turned off the lights, and went back to bed to a sleepless night.

Willie and Sebastian continued talking.

"Geez Willie, what do you think they meant about land development and some other thing that's coming?"

"I don't know. It doesn't sound good, but right now I want to go back down into our home."

"Home?"

"Yeah. The burrow, remember? The one you discovered? We'll make it our new home."

"I'm still not sure that's a good idea," Sebastian said with a worried look.

"Well, I am. Let's go. We need to explore."

So while Abigail tried to sleep, Sebastian and Willie went back down the burrow hole, now wide enough to accommodate Willie, and began to explore. What they found was a series of connecting burrows, each with an opening to different parts of the Newton property. Playing throughout the night, Sebastian and Willie chased one another, popping up first in the darkened garden, then by the pond, and finally along a pathway leading down some crooked steps. Willie had to widen each of the openings to get out. By sunrise the two had exhausted themselves, so they returned to the main room to sleep for the day.

At dusk, the kits again discussed remaining in the new burrow. Despite Sebastian's misgivings, Willie persuaded him to adopt the abandoned burrow as their new home, even without knowing what might have happened to the original owners.

~ 8 ~

Changing Habitats

Abigail entered her kitchen the next morning and poured a fresh cup of coffee. Absently sipping her hot coffee, she strolled over to the sliding glass doors. With a worried expression, she peered out into the backyard, still shrouded by morning fog. Of the many worries floating in her unconscious, she selected the destruction of her lawn, the least important of her concerns, as the subject upon which to dwell.

Abigail felt a growing tightness in her throat and struggled to keep angry tears from spilling as she began to think out loud. "Those holes in the backyard are still there from last summer's moles and voles. They're scattered all over the place. Those animals are dreadful. So destructive! The chipmunks aren't much better, but at least they're cute."

She covered her face with her hands and shook her head before continuing. "My thick smooth lawn. It's ruined, nothing more than a bumpy stumble. Even though I got rid of those critters last summer, I'll need to replant the lawn if I want it to be smooth again. It will cost a small fortune, one I can ill afford right now."

Still fretting over her lawn, Abigail walked to the kitchen island. After setting her coffee cup on the dark speckled top, she took a seat in one of the chairs facing the door. Her stress building, she stared at the empty seat across from her, the one DJ used to occupy every morning, and began talking as if he were sitting in the chair instead of sleeping upstairs.

"What am I supposed to do, honey? Now look, I can't even enjoy something as simple as my own back yard." She swallowed past the lump in her throat. "The lawn's been ruined."

Abigail's worries about her lawn were replaced by qualms about her spouse. His ever-changing personality and moods were disturbing. "It's part of the disease," she told herself, and turned her focus again toward the yard.

She watched a family of turkeys appear out of the fog. They marched awkwardly, with heads bobbing. One plopped down in the middle of the snap dragons as if to say between warbles, "Well, this is indeed a comfortable spot. Perhaps I'll stay a while."

Then she noted with dismay a deer dining on her roses in the butterfly garden. Momentarily their eyes met as the deer looked up from its grazing. Wearily, albeit with compassion for the hungry animals displaced by the construction, she sighed. "Yes, I understand, you need a place to live and eat, too, so go ahead."

The deer resumed its munching.

Abigail's backyard situation contained an element of irony. Just as the animals were inadvertently attacked by humans who destroyed their habitats, so too was her habitat under attack by the same lost and food-seeking animals.

"I can't do anything about the poor deer. But the bumpy lawn is my fault. If only I hadn't added the gardens, bird feeder, and pond. I thought tending the garden would be such a good hobby for DJ when he was forced to retire. How was I to know that feeding the birds in his haphazard manner and spilling seeds all over the ground would attract moles and voles? They certainly did make themselves at home in our backyard."

* * *

As part of the natural plan, Sebastian and Willie were genetically programmed to leave the burrow first thing each evening for Enlightenment School. The school was located in the southern sector of the woods, some distance from their new burrow and in the opposite direction of their old one. On the first day of school, both were nervous, Willie because of his previous experience in the Deep Creek School and Sebastian because, if the backpack didn't help him blend in, what then?

"We better get going or we'll be late," Willie said as he waited by the burrow entrance.

"I'm scared. At least you tried Enlightenment School in the Deep Creek before you came to live with us." Sebastian hoisted his new backpack onto his shoulders, the white stripes illuminated by the sun.

"You're right, and I remember what it was like being teased. Even though it was terrible, I learned how to avoid the mean kits. Now I have to start over, so I'm scared, too."

Mustering their courage, the two trotted off, faking an air of confidence. They came upon a small brook where Sebastian stopped. Staring over his shoulder at his image in the clear glasslike water, he attempted to reassure himself.

"I look just fine, as fine as can be with these new stripes. Mom said they're my safety stripes, and I should never take off my backpack."

It took Willie and Sebastian two hours to reach the school. It was an exceptionally large burrow with many chambers, each one housing a different Mephitidae class. Each class was led by a kit coach in charge of teaching lessons specific to that particular group of kits. A headmaster, elected by a majority vote of all the coaches, managed the day-to-day happenings in the school.

Although Willie hurried into his class, it took Sebastian longer to locate the correct room, because he peeked into each of the other classes, curious to learn more about his extended family. Sebastian spied minks, badgers, wolverines, and of course, the weasel class, where Willie was already seated in his designated spot, attentive to the kit coach who was busy taking attendance. Finally Sebastian entered his classroom, albeit somewhat tardy.

His skunk kit coach, known to all as Sir, motioned to Sebastian. "Please take a seat so we can get started. And oh, yes, you can leave your backpack in the closet."

Sebastian froze. His mother's words, "Never remove your backpack, it's you're protective shield," reverberated in his mind. He was conflicted, not knowing what to do. Sol and Sylvia had insisted that he always keep the backpack on, and he never questioned their judgment. However, they had also told him to listen carefully to his kit coach and obey all school rules.

Sir spoke up a bit louder this time. "Sebastian, we cannot begin until you remove your backpack. We don't have all day. Again, please place it in the closet."

Slowly, although he was going against the advice of his parents, Sebastian removed the feeble camouflage. Once it was off, a brief silence preceded the sound of a collective gasp surging from Sebastian's classmates. That single sound bounced not only against the exterior walls of the classroom, but also, and even more loudly, within the interior walls of Sebastian's subconscious. He felt small and worthless as all watched him slink to his desk.

At the end of the day Sebastian and Willie met outside the school entrance. "Hey Sebastian, where's your backpack?"

"I threw it in the trash. It didn't help. Fact is, I think it made things worse, just drawing attention to my stripelessness."

As they scampered back to their burrow, Sebastian told the whole story to Willie, who felt empathy, for he too was again teased for being so large. This school was no different. The kits were learning lessons all right.

"Our first day of school is over. Problem is, we have to go back tomorrow. All the other skunks have white badges of bravery running down their backs from their nose tips to their tail tips. The only ones who don't are the spots and the hoods, but at least they have each other and run together. All of them treat me like a loser."

"Listen Sebastian, I'm even bigger now than I was before, so I'm a loser too ... but not in the right way."

At dinner that night Sebastian and Willie stopped focusing on their problems and instead talked about their respective kit coaches.

"Mine's name is Sir and he's very strict. What about yours?"

"He looks a little like my old dad, but his eyes are very beady and intense."

"What's his name?"

"Everyone calls him Coach Politella."

"Did he teach anything?"

"Yeah, we had our first lesson and it was about the Three R's."

"Wow! Me, too. Sir reviewed the R of Respect not only for the Sacred Bundle, but also for oneself. Then he talked about the R of Resolution in achieving personal goals and the R of Responsibility. Willie, just how can we respect ourselves when we look so different from the pack?"

"I don't know, Sebastian, but we'll need to find a way."

* * *

Abigail put a batch of brownies in the oven and went into the family room where DJ was sitting on the couch looking at the paper. She sat down next to him.

"Well, DJ, at least the critters are gone. But their burrow holes are still all over the lawn and gardens. What do you think we should do?"

DJ continued looking at the paper and didn't respond.

"Please dear, put the paper down and try to concentrate. Now listen. You wanted the gardens, too, and agreed that I should hire a landscaper."

Abigail continued silently to herself, "And now you're so far away, you don't even seem to recognize the gardens. All you do is stare into space, talk to the squirrels, and look at the paper. I wish you could still talk to me. I miss you more than you can imagine. But—you can't imagine anymore!"

DJ looked at Abigail with a blank expression on his face and then, formulating words with difficulty, childishly repeated one of the rote phrases he had recently been using. "Abbey's eyes are brown and mine are blue."

"This is true, DJ, but it has nothing to do with the lawn."

Frustrated, Abigail smiled a sad smile and left the family room.

While DJ resumed looking at the newspaper, Abigail went upstairs to her office. She sat down in front of the computer, but couldn't concentrate. Her usually disciplined mind began to wander. She blocked out the looming issues facing her and returned to her problematic back yard.

The buzz, warning her that a door was open, interrupted Abigail's reverie. She dashed downstairs in response to the alarm she had recently installed because of DJ's increased wandering. It was the front door, and it was wide open. She forgot the yard, forgot her work, forgot the brownies baking in the oven. Her only concern was DJ. He was gone and she needed to find him.

"DJ? DJ! Where are you?"

Abigail ran back into the house, grabbed her keys, and backed the car out of the garage and down her steep driveway. Then she headed down the block, hoping to find DJ before he got more lost than he already was. By the time she found him, he was in the middle of the road, making his way up the steep grade with cars passing him and honking in warning as they went by. As she approached, one man had stopped and yelled out his car window, "What's the matter with you, mister? Are you nuts? Get out of the way or you'll get yourself killed!"

Quickly Abigail pulled over to the side of the road, put on the car's flashers, got out, and approached her husband in a gentle manner, saying, "Come on, honey. Let's go home."

DJ took Abigail's hand as if he were a small boy rather than a grown man. After she helped him into the car, they drove home in silence.

* * *

Sebastian and Willie were into their second week of school. Each sundown they left the safety and comfort of their burrow for the increasingly hostile atmosphere at Enlightenment School. Both began to dread school, despite their eagerness to learn the Three R's and find out how and when each would use their musk.

"Willie, I tried making friends with one of the white spotted skunks, but he avoids me and won't let me play in any of the group games."

"I've got problems, too, Sebastian. Every night I sit all alone during mid-meal. It makes me feel so anxious that I can hardly eat. And you know how much I love to eat. The only good news is that it's the best diet ever. I know I've lost weight because it's getting easier to wiggle into our burrow."

"What a horrible way to lose weight. At least you might begin to fit in. It's worse for me. I'll stick out no matter what."

"Unless we can find you stripes."

Discouraged, Sebastian answered, "Like where?"

"Something's bound to turn up. There has to be a solution to your problem."

"Don't forget about the trouble my Great[15] Grandfather Norton got into, trying to find a solution to the same problem."

"True, but we wouldn't be here today if it hadn't been for his mistake."

With reluctance and resignation Sebastian answered, "I know ... you're right."

"Because of your Great[15] Grandfather Norton, we're learning lessons at Enlightenment School, even if some are painful. Speaking of lessons, tell me what you learned today, because my stomach was growling the whole time Coach Politella was talking, and I wasn't paying attention. He went on and on about being responsible for something, but I'm not sure what else he said."

"Oh, yeah. Sir talked about it, too. Sounds like the lesson must have been the same in my class as yours since we both need to be responsible about how and when we use our musk. Sir said that my musk is used for a different purpose than yours."

"Like how?"

"Well, he said that male weasels use musk to mark their territory and that the female weasel uses her musk to attract a mate," Sebastian explained. "We skunks use our musk as a weapon."

"That's amazing. All this time I thought we were the same as far as our musk compartments go. Did Sir say how to make it work?"

"Nope. Not yet. He said first we need to understand when to use the musk before learning how to use it. That comes next week."

"Gee, it seems obvious. Shouldn't you use your musk whenever there's danger?"

"According to Sir, that isn't always an easy decision. There are only so many bullets—that's what Sir calls them— in our musk chamber, and it takes a while to reload. So if we decide incorrectly and then come up against an even greater enemy, we're doomed."

"Oh! I had no idea."

"Also, don't forget that the bullets are very powerful. Remember in the story how Great[15] Grandfather Norton was temporarily blinded? The skunks need to be extra careful when and how they use their bullets."

"Well, how do you decide?"

"Sir said we must consider every alternative first and shoot only if we must. He said something else, too."

"There's more?"

"Yup, the musk bullets should only be used to defend ourselves and those in our own family, no one else. He said it's part of being responsible."

Throughout the rest of the week and into the next, things did not improve at school. By the end of the third week, Sebastian told Willie, "Today my skunk-mates ganged up on me. One of the really popular skunks decked me and said I was spineless and unremarkable. I was fuming and almost shot him with one of my bullets, but it's illegal to shoot a relative. Then he and his friends started chanting, 'There goes stinky inky.' Another one yelled out, 'No he's spoiled oiled and lacquer luster.' I used to be proud of my thick shiny pelt. Mom always told me how beautiful my fur was. Now I know it was just her way of covering up the truth. I'm so ashamed. I hate myself. All the other skunks have stripes. Everyone has what I don't, marks of distinction. I'm tired of being different. I want real stripes!"

"Okay, okay, Sebastian. Now listen up. I've been thinking about your stripes...well, I mean your lack of stripes. I discovered a new road being built at the edge of the forest. It's completely black and there's a machine that comes along painting two white stripes on the blacktop as it rolls along. I think if you lie down flat on your belly, you'll blend into the road. No one will even notice that you're there and I was just thinking—"

"Willie," Sebastian interrupted excitedly. "I know where you're going with this. Wow, wouldn't that be fabulous? I could finally get stripes. Hurry, let's go now. Show me where it is."

So off they went, Willie in the lead and Sebastian, eager to keep up with his more experienced cousin, following close behind. Their scamper brought them to a road that was not far from their burrow.

"Well, here it is. Tell me what you think."

Sebastian's eyes grew wide. "It reminds me of myself, solid without any stripes—"

"Wait," Willie interrupted. "Do you hear what I hear? A humming sound? It's the striper and it'll be here soon. Quick, Sebastian. Go lie face down in the middle of the road. No one will see you. Come on, hurry! This is your big chance."

Sebastian did as Willie instructed. Lying flat in the middle of the road, he attempted to blend in until he felt at one with the road. His heart raced and his fur grew damp with anticipation as the humming sound grew closer. He held his breath. The next moment seemed to stretch out as far as the road itself and was about to take Sebastian in a direction he could never have imagined.

When Sebastian heard a loud roar emanating from the short, compact machine, he lost his nerve and attempted to get out of the way. Unfortunately his tail was pinned down by some gizmo on the apparatus and it was too late. Sebastian lay very still as the machine rolled within inches above him, spraying white paint on his tail, up and over his back, and then down his head. He continued to lie flat against the road even after the machine had long gone. When he felt a sharp pain coming from his tail, Sebastian began to quiver. All was quiet. Where was Willie?

As the pain in his tail gave way to a throbbing sensation, Sebastian cried out. "Willie, where are you? I think I'm hurt. Help me!"

Silence.

"Willie! Come here! I need you."

The silence continued.

Sebastian hollered, "Help!"

A few moments later, Sebastian felt the warmth of Willie's breath as well as his whiskers tickling his hind end, but still Willie said nothing. Then Sebastian heard Willie gasp, an indication that something was indeed terribly wrong.

"What is it, Willie? Do I have stripes or not?"

"Yes, well yes, cousin. You have two beautiful white stripes, but ..."

"But what?"

"Well, you've lost your tail. In short, you've become de-tailed by the machine and your posterior is bare and bleeding."

Sebastian made a harsh squealing sound, "Eeeeeee! What ... oh no, by the love of the sun, moon, and stars, how can that be? No tail?"

A horrified and guilty Willie grabbed some soft leaves lying at the edge of the forest and dabbed Sebastian's wounded hind end.

"The bleeding has stopped, but with the sky starting to drizzle, we'd better head back to our burrow. I'll figure out something along the way."

Willie picked up Sebastian's bushy tail, which was still lying on the road. Carrying it in his mouth, he began the trek home with a wounded and dejected Sebastian following close behind. The drizzle turned into a steady rain, which began to wash off the still wet stripes on Sebastian's back. Willie tried to protect the tail stripe but it, too, got wet. Just as the kits reached the side of the road, a northerly wind picked up, and the rain began to beat down harshly, creating a muddy rivulet gushing alongside the road.

Willie watched helplessly as the white paint drizzled from Sebastian's back, leaving his cousin's fur again without stripes.

"Oh, Sebastian, I am so dreadfully sorry for what has happened. I pledge to help you solve your now dual problem—no tail to speak of and still no stripes."

"What do you mean, no stripes?"

Sebastian looked down and with horror saw a white substance bubbling in the brown of the flowing stream, eddying in a downward path. His beautiful new stripes were disappearing with the rain.

At the bottom of the winding hill, the rushing water pooled in uneven recesses, forming puddles. They were muddy and slippery. Taking a misstep, Willie pitched sideways into the scrubby underbrush along the roadside. He came out yelping, his rain-matted fur covered with prickly burs on the left side of his body. As he attempted to pick one off, he felt stinging pain. But despite his efforts, the burs held fast.

"Sebastian, could you please try to loosen these stubborn burs gently and one by one? I wouldn't blame you if you refused to help me, but I can't do this alone."

Sebastian, who was still reeling from the recent loss of his tail and the ultimate failure of Willie's attempt to help him find stripes, was not feeling very sympathetic. Nonetheless, he went over to help his friend.

Pulling as gently as he could, Sebastian attempted to release a bur but it remained embedded in Willie's knotted fur.

"Okay, Willie. Gentle is not working, so get ready. This time I'm going to try harder."

Willie wrapped his arms around a nearby rock, bracing himself as Sebastian counted, "One, two, three ..."

Yanking as hard as he could on one of the larger protruding burs, Sebastian gave as great a tug as he could muster. However, the bur still refused to budge and the failed effort sent him lurching backwards. Willie, still holding onto the rock, lost his grip. Both kits tumbled down an embankment, where they landed side by side and unexpectedly attached at the hip, Willie's left to Sebastian's right, in a tangle caused by the obstinate burs.

When Willie tried to stand, Sebastian gave out a yelp, and started to struggle. "Oh! Ow! Stop!"

"Sebastian, wait! Don't move! I think we're stuck on each other!"

Still reeling from the recent tail trauma, Sebastian felt dizzy and sick. "Stuck? Whadya mean, stuck?"

"Attached together."

Sebastian groaned, "But how?"

"It's the burs. We can't move by ourselves. We can only move together."

As the kits worked to right themselves, they realized the only way to get back to their burrow was to move as if they were Siamese twins. So with Willie carrying Sebastian's tail in his mouth and Sebastian sporting a bare hind end, they synchronized their paw steps and slowly made their way back through the woods.

"Sebastian you're going too slow. It's tripping me up."

With difficulty Sebastian answered, "Can't help it, too much pain."

"Okay, I'll slow down. But at this rate we'll never make it to the lady's house."

"Lady's house?"

"Yeah, the people house in front of our burrow."

Heaving, Sebastian said, "Why there? I wanna go home."

"Sebastian, you need more help than I can give you. Maybe the lady can help."

So en route, Willie convinced Sebastian that the only solution was to seek out the lady who lived in the people house.

~ 9 ~

Abigail Meets New Neighbors

Abigail could hear the alarm of the smoke detectors as she drove up the driveway and into the garage. She hurried around to help DJ out of the passenger side of the car, then gripping his hand tightly, tugged him along behind her. When she reached for the alarm keypad just beside the door into the basement, she punched in the code to cancel the alarm and opened the door in time to hear the phone ringing. Out of breath and huffing, Abigail grabbed the receiver. In response to the alarm company's inquiry she said, "No, don't send a fire truck. We're fine now. It's just smoke, I burned some brownies. Thanks for the call."

After hanging up the phone, she helped DJ up the basement stairs. Because of his increasing difficulty walking, it might just as well have been a mountain. Once in the family room Abigail seated DJ in front of the TV, put in a video, and opened the windows to fan out the thick smoke. Returning to the kitchen, she removed the charred brownies from the oven and dumped them into the sink. Watching the might-have-been yummy brownies being ground away by the garbage disposal, she thought about DJ's decline and her plight with him.

DJ passively sat watching an old OSU football game their sons had taped many happy years ago. This was the third time in the past week DJ had wandered away from the house. Abigail knew she finally needed to hire a daytime companion for him.

With a deep sigh, she joined DJ on the couch. "That was close. Too bad about the brownies, though. I'll make you another batch later, honey."

Though Abigail felt sleepy, she was worried that DJ might try to escape again so she repositioned herself, lying down with her legs across his lap as a preventive measure. She had just begun to doze off when she was aroused by a tapping noise coming from the kitchen. She blinked the drowsiness out of her eyes, glanced at DJ who was sleeping soundly, and carefully disengaged her legs from his lap.

Abigail tiptoed toward the kitchen. With each step, the tapping sound became more pronounced until she was facing the clear glass of the kitchen patio doors. When Abigail peered out, she saw two animals, both muddy, full of burs, and attached side by side, one to the other. One of them looked to her like a skunk but didn't have stripes, which she found most curious. The other she recognized as a weasel.

Speaking softly she said, "Hmmm. I bet you're the animals who knocked over the trash can a couple weeks ago. Definitely not raccoons."

Abigail, who had no fear of animals, slid the door open and stepped out to have a better look. What she saw were two bedraggled animals. It was then that Abigail noticed the tail of another animal in the mouth of the weasel.

"Must have been quite a fight, huh?"

Willie gazed into Abigail's eyes. She held his gaze.

"No? Then, where did it come from?"

Willie added a few squeaks, trying to communicate what had happened, but Abigail didn't understand him, yet. Then she squatted down to examine the two more closely.

"You poor animals. Where on Earth did all those burs come from? And how ever did you get stuck together like this?"

Willie, made more noises, modulating the tone of his squeals, while Sebastian began to whimper. As always when communicating with a new animal, Abigail paid close attention to each, trying to discern their distinct language.

It had started in grade school. One day Abigail found she had the ability to understand and be understood by her beloved Golden Retriever, aptly named Goldie. As she grew into her teens, her ability to communicate with animals developed to include other dogs, cats, horses, birds, and even a frog named Sudrick. Ultimately, the subject of animal telepathy so intrigued Abigail that she read and took courses on the subject, practiced its methodology, and became proficient. Her interests expanded into not only listening to animal pets, but also to wild animals and all beings of life, including trees, flowers, and the Earth itself.

"Say, little one, you're whimpering," said Abigail. "Show me where it hurts."

Sebastian let out a single weak moan, turned his head as best he could and looked behind in the direction of his tail. Abigail took a look at Sebastian's rear and was horrified.

"Oh, no! For heaven's sake, you've lost your tail. And the fur around your behind is all matted with dried blood."

The animals both began making noises, hoping that Abigail understood.

"So, weasel, is that the skunk's tail in your mouth?"

Willie answered in two squeaks which Abigail translated to be uh-huh.

"Then there wasn't a fight?"

This time Willie answered in squeaks of a different tone and moved his furry head from side to side.

"Well, maybe you'll be able to explain later. Right now what you need is medical attention. I've had plenty of experience with all kinds of animals, but your problems are greater than I can handle. I need to get you to my vet."

Willie and Sebastian didn't understand "vet," but they could feel Abigail's genuine concern and knew they had come to the right place.

"Listen, you two. Don't go anywhere."

Willie licked his lips, Sebastian made a smacking sound, and both were shivering.

"Okay, I get it. You're hungry, thirsty, and cold. I'll be right back with food, water, and a cover to keep you warm."

* * *

After Abigail left Willie and Sebastian, wet and shivering outside her door, she ran inside to fetch a faded patchwork quilt and some nourishment. Returning, she set a few pellets of Oliver's dog food and a bowl of water in front of the animals. When they were finished chewing and lapping, she scooped them up with the quilt and folded it over them.

Sebastian and Willie could feel the softness of the quilt and its pleasant scent. Instantly they felt surrounded by warmth and protection. Abigail placed Sebastian and Willie in one of Oliver's cages, went into the family room to fetch DJ, and holding the cage in one hand and DJ's hand in the other, she went down the steps to the garage. Next she placed the cage in the back of the car, helped DJ into the front, and called Murphy's Animal Hospital on her cell phone as she backed out of the drive.

"Hi, Susie. It's Abbey. I need to see Dr. Murphy right away. It's an emergency... No, Oliver's fine. It's two animals—long story. I'll be there in fifteen minutes and explain."

As Abigail rushed to the vet, Sebastian and Willie felt the bumping, swaying, and forward movement of the car. Each time Sebastian's hind end banged against the cage, he squealed in pain.

Willie tried to comfort him. "Oh, Sebastian, I'll bet that hurt. I'm so sorry, sorry about everything."

Willie continued, "It'll be okay, Sebastian. I can tell this lady likes us. She seems to know just what to do, and right now we need to be taken care of."

With a sudden jerking movement, the car came to an abrupt halt. The hatchback of the car popped open. As gently as she could, Abigail slid the cage out of the car and into the open air, then walked around to the passenger side with the cage swaying back and forth.

"Here we are, DJ. Let me help you out so we can get these animals into Jack's office."

Jack Murphy had been the family vet ever since Oliver was a pup. "This is a tall order, Abbey. It won't be easy to repair the skunk's tail."

"Jack, I know you'll do your very best. Even if you can't reattach his tail, I hope you'll be able to save him. He looks so weak. After all, you are a miracle worker. Remember the time Oliver was hit by a car? He never would have survived if it hadn't been for you. Poor, uh...I think his name is Sebastian."

"Sebastian?"

"Yes, that's the skunk's name. And wait a minute, it's coming to me. The weasel is Willie."

"Abbey, I won't even ask. You never fail to amaze me. While you're here, I have a nasty cat I want you to have a chat with. Name's Buster."

"No, problem, just point me in his direction."

"Third cage on the feline side of the kennel. Go have a look while I tend to Sebastian and Willie. Meet me back here in about half an hour.

"Can DJ stay in the waiting room while I take a look at Buster?"

"Absolutely. And Susie can keep an eye on him."

When Abigail returned to the office, albeit with a few scratch marks on her arms, she said, "Boy, you're right. That Buster is quite a tomcat. Very aggressive, but I had him eating out of my hand by the time I was finished. How'd you do with Sebastian and Willie? Any recommendations?"

"Yes, let me review my medical treatment plans. For starters, they're being bathed in a special solution to soften the burs, which need to be removed so the animals can be separated. The technician will need to use tweezers to get them all out. Next, an antibiotic salve will be applied to any open areas, and then I'll give them a series of shots.

"How long will it take?"

"Probably a couple of hours."

"Okay, but after you're done, keep their cages together. They've become codependent."

"Whatever you say, I'll call and give you an update before considering a surgical reattachment of the skunk's... uh... Sebastian's tail."

Dr. Murphy escorted Abigail out of the examining room and back into the waiting room where DJ sat with a newspaper in front of his face.

"Thanks, Susie. I can always count on you. Come on, DJ. We can go home now."

One of Dr. Murphy's technicians bathed Willie and Sebastian in a warm solution before attempting to extract the burs that caused their physical attachment. Once that was accomplished, another technician came in, and each worked separately on the animals to remove the remaining burs. Willie yelped, squealed, and squirmed as each bur was loosened and pulled out, but Sebastian only moaned, too weak to do anything in response. After this ordeal they were rubbed all over with a smelly cream, and Dr. Murphy came in to give them a series of shots. When the doctor had finished, he gave Abigail a call.

"Hi, Abbey. Jack Murphy here."

"Hi, Jack, I've been waiting for your call. How are the animals?"

"Willie's tired, but fine. It was easier to remove the burs from Willie than from Sebastian, but the technician got them all."

"What about Sebastian?"

"He lost a lot of blood and is still very weak. The burs on his back were too tangled for the technician to remove. I had to shave them off myself."

"Wow. That's really drastic. Will his fur grow back?"

"Yes, in time. I also had to use a special liniment on Sebastian to wash away a white residue, probably paint, that was on his back and his detached tail."

"Tell me more about his tail."

"Well, it's in the cold storage tank until surgery."

"So, you're going to try? Do you think it'll work?"

"Can't say for sure and there are the usual risks, but there's a good chance the procedure will be successful...Listen, Abbey. I found something very interesting about Sebastian. After all the burs and paint were removed, I combed through the tail before putting it into the storage tank. The animal is indeed rare, being the opposite of an albino and seemingly without a hint of stripes. But I noticed just a few white hairs at his hind end as well as on the root end of his tail. It might just be the rudiments of stripes."

"My heavens, that's incredible. Do you think Sebastian might develop stripes?

"Only time will tell. I did some research, but found next to nothing on the subject of stripeless skunks. We'll just need to wait and see what happens when his fur grows back."

"By the way, I've been meaning to ask you, how's DJ? Did the neurologist ever come up with a diagnosis?"

Abigail froze. The diagnosis was not one she readily voiced. It was so hard having to tell everyone, saying it repeatedly to relatives on both sides of the family and to their many friends, some as close as next door and others scattered all over the country. Now, she was being asked yet another time. A large lump swelled in her throat, making it difficult to speak. She hesitated before answering.

"Are you still there, Abbey?"

"Yes...yes, Jack." Her voice cracked and was hesitant, "I'm here, but I'm afraid DJ isn't."

"What do you mean?"

"Well, his neurologist said it's probable Alzheimer's disease."

"Oh, Abbey, my dear friend. Alzheimer's disease. How horrible. I'm so sorry for you both. Did they say how long he's expected to live?"

"From ten to twenty years since he's so young, only fifty-four."

"That's quite a sentence, let me know if there's anything I can do to help."

"Sure. Thanks, Jack." Attempting to regain her composure, Abigail changed the subject. "When will you schedule surgery on the tail?"

"Well, I know this is soon, but can you come back in now? I don't want to delay the surgery."

"Jack, I'm on my way."

* * *

Willie was in a state of near panic. Sebastian's unresponsiveness magnified his fear, worry, and guilt. He began to mutter.

"I was the one who gave Sebastian such a dangerous idea, but he was just so miserable, and what with me losing weight, and him still without any stripes—please in the name of our Great Grandfathers to the Fifteenth Power of Greats, let Sebastian be okay."

Suddenly Willie's prayers were interrupted by the sound of Dr. Murphy's voice in the outer office. When he heard the doctor mention Abigail's name, his ears perked up.

Hearing parts of the phone conversation, Willie was able to piece together some of the sentences and come to several conclusions, some correct, others not.

"... tail in cold storage tank ..." Willie thought it meant they were able to clean and save Sebastian's tail. That sounded like a good thing.

"... surgical procedure will be successful ..." Surgery! That sounded dangerous to Willie.

"...a few white hairs ..." Could it be that Sebastian was developing stripes?

"... How's DJ doing..." Willie was right, something was wrong with Abbey's mate.

"... diagnosis of Alzheimer's disease..." Astounded, Willie was certain Dr. Murphy said Old Hamster's Disease. He was reminded of what happened on the Isles of Ill in *Die Alten Tage*, and his imagination began to spin out of control. Willie was still in a state of shock when the technician came in to get Sebastian who was sedated and in a deep sleep. Gently removing Sebastian from his cage, the technician placed him in a small box-like container and carried Sebastian away.

Already in a frenzied state, Willie knew that something serious was about to happen to Sebastian. He began to make a gurgling sound in his throat, but it drew no attention. Then when he tried to make it louder, the sound turned into a shrill cry.

Abigail had just returned and was in the waiting room, eager to find out where surgery would take place, when she heard the shrill cry coming from the kennel.

Susie, who had been scheduling an appointment, put down the phone. "Hey Abbey! Sebastian is being prepped for surgery."

"Listen, Susie. Do you hear that high pitched animal sound? I know it's Willie, trying to get my attention. He must be very worried about Sebastian. Can I go back to his cage?"

"Sure but don't spend too much time or you'll miss the beginning of Sebastian's surgery."

"I'll just be a minute."

Abigail hurried through the waiting room door to the long hallway leading to the kennel. At the far end of the feline wing, there was a food pantry where Abigail scooped out a few food pellets before finding Willie, who was huddled and trembling in the back corner of his cage.

"Willie, I'm nervous, too. But Dr. Murphy has assured me that everything will be fine."

Not certain that her words alone would calm him, Abigail chanced something that was absolutely forbidden. She put her fingers between the bars and then squeezed her hand sideways until it was inside the cage. She beckoned the weasel to come near.

Willie moved cautiously from the back to Abigail's extended hand. First he explored with his whiskers, touching each knuckle. Then when Abigail opened her hand revealing a few food pellets, he began to nibble. He felt comforted by her offering and after chewing and swallowing each of the pellets, Willie lingered, licking Abigail's hand.

The touch of his whiskers tickled, making Abigail giggle, something she hadn't done in a very long time. She found Willie's soft brown fur comforting. Each was able to relax, with the help of the other.

Now that Abbey was in a quiet place with Willie, she could tune into his thoughts.

"Abbey, thanks for being my friend. I'm so scared."

Abigail then spoke directly to Willie. "Willie, I will always be your friend. Sebastian's, too. Thank you for speaking directly to me. That takes trust."

Though surprised that she understood him so well, Willie accepted her unusual ability, and the two began the first of many conversations.

"I'm worried about what I heard Dr. Murphy say."

"What did you hear?"

Willie did not broach the subject of DJ's Old Hamster's Disease. Instead he said, "I heard him say surgery, and I know that Sebastian's life is at stake."

"Yes, Willie that's true. Surgery is dangerous. But Dr. Murphy has performed many animal surgeries, and his clinic is one of the few animal hospitals in the region. It's got all the latest equipment. I feel confident that Sebastian will not only live through the surgery, but that he'll have his tail back again, too. Dr. Murphy told me Sebastian's scent glands are undamaged. Once his tail is reattached, he can use it to fan his ... well, I'll just call it 'fumes.' Of course, Sebastian will require exercise and practice to help strengthen his tail muscles after the repair heals. Now listen, I need to hurry so I can keep an eye on the surgery. I'll come back when it's over and let you know how Sebastian is doing."

"How long will it take?"

"I'm not sure, but it may be a while. Try to relax. Think of favorite things and all the fun times you and Sebastian have had and just how much fun you'll continue to have."

"I'll try, but hurry back the minute it's over. Promise?"

"Promise."

Abigail gave Willie one more pat, and drew her hand out from between the cage bars. Then she headed for the surgical suite where Dr. Murphy greeted her.

"Sebastian is all prepped and ready. Wendy just brought him in. Go ahead and get scrubbed, masked, and gowned."

Wendy placed Sebastian stomach down on the small operating table, which was well padded and draped in white. A large fluorescent light illuminated the table. All the necessary instruments were covered and ready in a tray that was attached to a swing arm beside the operating table. Abigail returned, garbed in scrubs fashioned out of a cotton

print depicting cartoon dogs and cats, rather than
the usual drab blue.

"Ready?"

"Ready!"

Jack Murphy masterfully wielded the scalpel,
thread, and needle. Wendy stood by with antiseptic sponges, circular needles, and surgical thread.
Abigail observed.

Sebastian had been anesthetized and remained
unconscious throughout the operation. Dr. Murphy
first removed any small hairs that still remained in
the shaved skin around the tail end. Then he scraped
the area, following with a liberal application of
alcohol. Next Dr. Murphy quickly stitched tail to
hind end with small neat sutures.

"Now closing. Alcohol swab... gauze... packing...
bandages, please."

And with that, it was over. Sebastian's tail was
reattached, and a tight bandage around his hind end
protected the incision. Abigail hurried back to the
kennel, anxious to report back to Willie.

"It's over, Willie. The surgery went well. Sebastian's in recovery and sleeping peacefully until the
anesthesia wears off."

Willie's questions came in rapid succession. "Did
it work? Is his tail reattached? When can I see him?"

"Willie, slow down. Take a deep breath. Yes, Dr.
Murphy was able to repair his tail but it's bandaged
up for now. We probably won't be able to see him
until tomorrow.

"Okay, but then what happens?"

"According to Dr. Murphy, Sebastian needs physical therapy to strengthen the muscles around his tail. It could take a couple of months before he's completely healed."

"But ... where will Sebastian live while he's healing? I don't know how to take care of him."

"That's a good question, and one I've been pondering. I think it's best if you both come live with me and DJ. That is, at least until Sebastian's tail is completely healed."

"You mean leave our burrow? Live in your house?"

"Yes," Abigail explained. "I know it sounds difficult, but this way you won't be separated."

Willie looked uncomfortable at the thought, "But I want to go home to our cozy burrow behind your house."

"If you go back to your burrow, you'll be separated from Sebastian. I'd like you both to become part of our household, as pets. Just like Oliver. Of course, first you need to learn the rules of the house."

Willie began to think about how he and Sebastian had been chased by Oliver. He wondered how they would ever be able to live in the same household. But then, Willie's thoughts of Oliver were interrupted by something very different—the recollection of what happened to the two hamsters from the Isles of Ill who had been captured by hunters, taken as pets, and then abandoned when they became old or sick and left to harden and die on the Isle.

Although Willie knew he wasn't related to the hamster family, the suggestion that he and Sebastian become pets was alarming. Maybe it would be okay, though. This was the opposite of the story about the Isles of Ill. Abbey found them *after* they were sick and wanted to adopt them anyway. "Willie, I can hear your worries in my mind. What is this Isles of Ill that makes you so afraid?" Abigail asked.

"It's a long story and might even involve DJ."

"How? What can DJ possibly have to do with this?"

"Well, it wasn't on purpose, but I overheard Dr. Murphy when you told him about DJ having Old Hamster's Disease."

"Old Hamster's Disease?"

"Yes, that's the very disease the pet hamsters got once they were abandoned on the Isles of Ill. We learned about it from a chapter in our ancestral saga, *Die Alten Tage*."

"Did you say '*Die Alten Tage*'?"

"Yes, that's it. The ancient history book of the Skunk and Weasel family."

"I think '*Die Alten Tage*' is German for *The Olden Days*. Willie, you must tell me what happened in *The Olden Days*."

"All I can tell you is that our Great[15] Grandfathers, and that's a very long time ago, were best friends. Sebastian's Great[15] Grandfather was the chemist who developed skunk stink and my Great[15] Grandfather invented the raft the skunks used to escape from Westphalia."

"Escape from what?"

"Their homeland. The skunks were expelled because Sebastian's Great[15] Grandfather Norton polluted the forest when he discovered the chemical solution for skunk stink."

"Chemical solution?"

"Yeah, Norton Bulymur—that's his name—was the first one to be born without stripes, and he had this lab where he was always experimenting to find a solution for his stripelessness. Bubo the Owl, the mean leader of the forest, rounded up the chiefs of the animal tribes and persuaded them to banish all the skunks after an explosion happened in Norton's lab."

"There was an explosion?"

"Yup. A bad one. That's what caused the pollution in the forest. Anyway, they escaped and found a new home in America."

"How did they escape?"

"Well, like I said, my Great[15] Grandfather Mordecai Wilhelm invented an escape raft."

"Wilhelm, huh? Ah, so that's who you're named after. Then what happened?"

"They found a new homeland. Norton established a school and the skunks and weasels multiplied throughout Penn's Wood and all over."

"Where is this book, *Die Alten Tage*?"

"Our parents keep it behind their burrow, hidden under a knothole in a decaying tree branch. It's all wrapped up and covered with leaves for protection."

"Willie, after all this is over and Sebastian is healed, both of you are free to return to your burrow, but I'm very interested in the history of your family. Do you think you and Sebastian might share the book with me? Perhaps let me read it?"

"I don't know. It's written in an ancient language that only Embla can translate."

"Embla? Who's that?"

"Oh, Abbey, it's just too hard to explain, but Sebastian can tell you the whole story once he's up to it. Besides, I'm worried because we've already missed several classes of Enlightenment School."

"Enlightenment School? What is Enlightenment School?"

"It's the school that Norton founded. When Mephitidae kits are about a year old, they need to leave their parent's den and forage for themselves, eventually finding a new home. We kits go from year one, called the Year of Pretendment, to year two, called the Year of Enlightenment. We go to a special Enlightenment School where we learn the ways of our Mephitidae family."

"Oh, wow! That is so interesting. I'd like to hear the details later, but first we need to discuss my home rules."

"Hmmm." Willie thought about the Three R's that he and Sebastian were learning about at Enlightenment School. "We have rules, too. They have to do with behavior, and we must abide by them."

"What are they, Willie?"

"The Three Rs of Respect, Responsibility, and Resolution. I guess you could say they're the Mephitidae family rules."

"Amazing, simply amazing. I can hardly believe what I'm hearing. Those are the same Three R's my mother taught me when I was growing up. DJ and I instilled them in our two sons, too."

"Wow, that's really something. We both have the same Three R's to live by."

"If only it were that simple! But if you agree to come live with us, you can still continue learning your Three R's and how they apply in the Newton household. Do you agree to join Sebastian and come live with us? I promise that becoming our pets has nothing to do with DJ's illness."

"So DJ is sick with, with ...?"

"Alzheimer's disease." But even though Abigail said Alzheimer's disease, Willie still heard "Old Hamster's disease."

"I knew it, I just knew it!" Willie gasped for a second time.

He pondered a bit before agreeing to become a pet in the Newton household. What else could he do? He didn't want to abandon Sebastian. So he agreed to settle into the Newton household and become Abigail's personal pet.

Over the next month, Sebastian regained the weight he lost, and his eyes were again bright and alert with curiosity. Even the bald spots on his back had stubbles of hair growth.

Sebastian's favorite place to nap during his recuperation was on DJ's lap, where DJ would instinctively reach down to tenderly pet his new little friend. It took until the end of the summer to establish inseparable bonds between the animals and their owners, Willie with Abigail and Sebastian with DJ. By the time their roles as household pets had been fully established, Sebastian's fur was growing in and with some surprising results. As for Oliver, the earlier animosity towards the kits subsided as he became the special friend of the Davey-sitter.

The kits saw one another sporadically throughout the day, starting each morning after breakfast. DJ took a long nap with Sebastian curled up on his lap, while Abigail's routine included a shower and washing her hair. Willie would wait patiently outside her bathroom door until she came out and then follow her downstairs to the kitchen for coffee.

But today Abigail was in a hurry. "It's getting late, and I've got to get to this meeting on time," she said, glancing at her watch.

"Meeting? What's it about?"

"A new zoning ordinance in my borough. The officials are going to explain it. From what I hear, it's very complicated."

Willie followed Abigail as she went down the stairs to the basement level and then out to the garage. He was puzzled about the new words—zoning, ordinance and complicated.

"I'll ask Abbey about it when she gets back," he told himself, "but right now I've got to find Sebastian. There's so much to tell him, especially about DJ having Old Hamster's Disease. He needs to be warned. And now is the perfect time since Abbey's on her way to a meeting and will be away for a while."

~ 10 ~

Sunshine & Shadows

Sebastian was asleep, comfy within the crook of DJ's arm, when Willie entered DJ's bedroom.

"Wake up! I need to talk to you."

As Sebastian stirred, DJ stretched his right arm, releasing Sebastian from his grip.

"Come on Sebastian! Jump down. There's something important I need to tell you. Abbey's not home, so we have time to talk privately."

"That's perfect, Willie, because I have something to tell you, too. You're in for the surprise of a lifetime! Something's happening that you won't believe!"

Willie, nervous about what he had to tell Sebastian, said, "Okay, Sebastian, since you're so excited, you go first."

"Ready for this? The fur on my back and head— you know, where it was shaved off before the operation—well, it's beginning to grow in. And guess what? I think some of it might be white."

"That's amazing! How do you know?"

"Yesterday I was outside in the gardens with DJ. When he sat in the grass beside the pond, I sat on a rock right next to him. He started petting my back and saying, 'Good Unk.' That's what he calls me. While I was sitting there, a ray of sunshine bounced off my back and into the pond. I caught a glimpse of myself in the reflection, and I was so stunned I could hardly breathe. I saw two thin lines of white fur going down my back."

"Let me take look." Willie led Sebastian to a window where the light was better. "Yup, there they are! The beginnings of two paths of white fuzz growing on your tail and back."

"Willie, do you think it's possible? Dad said this is the Age of Aquarius, a time when an ordinary skunk like me, born without stripes, has the opportunity to earn them."

"Don't you get it yet, Sebastian?"

"Get what?"

"There's nothing ordinary about you. Because you look different and you are different from all the other skunks, so you're already special."

"Thanks, Willie. You're the only one who thinks so besides Mom, Dad, and now Abigail, and maybe DJ. If this truly happens then it'll be me who has a chance to free future generations from the stripeless curse that's plagued the skunk families for eons."

"Yes, I do think it's possible."

"But why?"

"When we were in the kennel, I overheard parts of a conversation between Abbey and Dr. Murphy. He told Abbey that, after all the burs were cleaned off your back and tail, he noticed a few white hairs both at your hind end and your tail root. So maybe your stripes are finally going to develop."

"That would be a miracle! But I don't understand. Dad said the stripes had to be earned. What have I done?"

"I'm not sure, but there's other stuff I need to tell you, things you don't know about."

"Like what?"

"I don't want to talk here. Let's go somewhere away from DJ and his new friend. What does Abbey call him?"

"I think she calls him the Davey-sitter."

"Yes, away from him."

Willie led the way down the steps to the laundry room where they hid behind the warm furnace.

"Now it's your turn, Willie. What do you need to tell me that's so important?"

Willie whispered, "DJ's sick, really sick."

"Sick? With what?" Sebastian asked loudly.

"Shhh! I don't want anyone to hear."

"Sick with what?" Sebastian whispered.

Willie was hesitant, "Well, it's so hard to say."

"Come on, Willie, tell me."

"DJ has Old Hamster's Disease."

"No! That can't be! DJ is definitely not a hamster. And he isn't a pet either, so you must be wrong."

"I know it's strange, but it's true."

"How do you know?"

"Abbey told me."

"Oh, no! If he really has Old Hamster's Disease and if it's the same as the hamsters in the Isles of Ill, he'll harden and die. What'll I do without him? I need him as much as he needs me. I knew something was wrong, but I never imagined the possibility of Old Hamster's Disease. You know, except for the times I'm in his lap, he runs around in circles all over the house saying, 'Help me, help me, help me.' It's so bad Abbey can't even get him to sit down for a meal. Lately she has to chase him around with a spoon, trying to get him to take even one bite. And he's been losing weight."

"Sebastian, Maybe DJ's being zapped."

"Zapped?"

"Yes. Remember in the Isles of Ill when the pets kept getting zapped by those strange branch endings?"

"I forgot about that. Isn't that how they hardened?"

"Right. And that's why the Isles got too heavy to float."

"And then they sank. The whole world sank." Puzzled, Sebastian scratched his head. "But DJ isn't getting heavier, he's losing weight. Maybe if he hardens, our whole world will sink."

"True, but you said DJ relaxes when you're in his lap. So maybe that's healing him. And have you ever considered that DJ's petting might be the reason your fur is growing back so quickly?"

"No. But you might be right. Perhaps his rubbing is stimulating my fur."

"That makes sense. Maybe the petting is helping your hair grow faster."

"Yeah!"

"But that doesn't explain the two paths of white growing in your fur. That still remains a mystery."

Sebastian rubbed his forehead. "It is strange."

"Sebastian, something just occurred to me. Do you remember in the Isles of Ill when Mousella wanted to help the hamsters?"

"Yes."

"Well, maybe you have a chance to do what Mousella couldn't."

"Whadya mean?" Sebastian asked.

"I think you are DJ's pet. After all, he does pet you and that may be helping him. I'm certain your friendship is worthy of earning one of your stripes."

"One stripe? Why only one?"

"Because one good deed, the way I figure, counts for one white stripe. Since two paths are growing, there must be another good deed you're meant to accomplish before you become a full-fledged striped skunk and dispel your family curse."

"Good reasoning, Willie. A second good deed ... hmmm ... what could it be?"

Willie answered, "I'm not sure, but, give me time, I'll figure it out."

The kits, weary from worry, curled up next to each other and settled in for a nap. They dozed until the grind of the garage door woke them.

"Sebastian, wake up. Abbey's home."

The two scampered out from behind the furnace and headed for the door. Sitting next to one another, they awaited Abigail's entrance. When she opened the door, she practically tripped over them.

"Why hello, you two. And you're greeting me the moment I walk into the house because ...?"

"Abbey, I've explained everything to Sebastian and we all need to talk."

"What do you mean, explained everything?"

"I told Sebastian about DJ's Old Hamster's Disease."

She turned to regard Sebastian. "Oh, Sebastian, I'm so sorry I didn't explain this to you sooner, but I wanted to wait until you recovered from surgery. We're all afraid of what's happening to DJ's mind and body."

"Abbey, isn't there something that can make him get better?"

"No, Willie. Not yet. Millions of dollars have been spent looking for ways to prevent, stop, or reverse Alzheimer's disease, or as you call it, Old Hamster's Disease. But so far nothing's been discovered. Researchers keep looking for a solution. They've experimented in their labs using all kinds of chemicals and chemical combinations, with little success. Anyway, the best medicine so far only slows the disease."

"What good is that? He's still sick and getting worse."

"You're so right, Sebastian, and lately it's a question I've been asking myself, too."

Again, Willie inserted himself into the conversation. "I wish I could do something to help, like Sebastian is."

"Helping? How? What's Sebastian doing?"

"He lets DJ pet him."

"Yeah, when I sit in his lap and DJ pets me, he relaxes," Sebastian explained.

"Are you sure? That's incredible! Even the strongest medications can't seem to do that."

"And Abbey, get this. At the same time I'm helping DJ, he's helping me!"

"But Sebastian, I don't understand."

"The petting. I think it stimulates the hair on my back."

"You could be right. I noticed your fur is growing back quicker than expected."

"And Abbey," Willie added, "did you notice that two paths are growing down Sebastian's back and tail?"

"Yes, I certainly did. Dr. Murphy saw some white hairs on his tail and hind end and told me Sebastian's stripes might still develop."

"You know what, Abbey? I think Sebastian's developing one of his stripes as a reward for being DJ's friend."

"Just one of his stripes? What about the other one? There are two fuzzy white paths."

"True, but like I told Sebastian, so far he's only done one good deed, even though it is very special and very wonderful."

"Hmmm, yes. You do have a point. But what does doing good deeds have to do with Sebastian growing stripes?"

"It's about the prophecy, Abbey."

"What prophecy? What are you talking about?"

"According to skunk lore, during the astrological Age of Aquarius, one special skunk, born of no stripes, will be given the opportunity to earn them. This skunk will rise above all others and forge two remarkable pathways for all skunkdom. When this happens, the curse of stripelessness will be erased from the skunk family forever."

"Wow! A prophecy and, come to think of it, we are in the Age of Aquarius. Willie, do you have any ideas about what this other accomplishment might be?"

"Not at the moment, but even though I'm not an inventor like my Great[15] Grandfather Mordecai, I am inventive. And I owe it to Sebastian to help him figure it out."

"That's very noble of you, Willie."

"I don't see it as noble. It's my fault he lost his tail."

"Willie, the fact that you're taking responsibility is the first step into your passage from weasel kit into an adult ermine."

"What's that?"

"It's the winter you."

"I like my name, why do I need to become a Herman?"

"Not Herman. Ermine. Instead of weasel brown, your fur will become a beautiful snowy white in the winter, and this winter you'll be of adult ermine age."

"Wow!" Willie exclaimed.

"After all, white hair signals the possibility of acquired wisdom, at least it does for humans. Also, don't forget that Sebastian had a choice, and he chose unwisely when he agreed to participate in the stripe caper."

"True."

"Now Sebastian, listen to me carefully," Abbey said. "Part of your growing up and maybe even earning that second stripe may have to do with making the right choices."

"How will I know when there's something important enough that my choice will make a real difference? You know, be worthy of a second stripe?"

"You'll know by instinct, Sebastian. The harder part may be in the choice itself."

"Why?"

"Because if the choice isn't clear then it becomes a dilemma."

"Okay, I guess I'll just have to wait until whatever it is I'm supposed to do comes to me."

"That's correct."

Willie interrupted, "Abigail, who is Emma?"

"Emma?"

"Yeah, you said something about Emma when you were explaining to Sebastian about making choices."

"It's dilemma, not Emma."

"So exactly what is dilemma?"

"It's something that happens when both choices you can make are right and wrong at the same time."

"So if that happens, what should I do?" Sebastian asked.

"Then you must study both sides and make the best decision based on your knowledge and experience."

"But how am I supposed to get knowledge and experience?"

"Well, Willie mentioned that you were both attending a special school before your accident. I promised Willie that after your tail healed and you regained your health, the two of you could return to your burrow and go back to school. Perhaps it's time."

"Leave here?"

"Yes. I wish you both could live with me and DJ forever but there are lessons to be learned, in school and in life, before you can make important decisions, the kind that will earn that second stripe."

"Will we ever see you and DJ again?"

"Of course! You're both part of my family, and you'll always be welcome here."

Then Willie asked, "So Abbey, when do you think we should leave?"

"Probably soon. You've already missed about eight weeks of school."

"Sebastian, I guess now would be as good a time as ever.

"Okay, Willie, but first let's say goodbye to DJ"

~ 11 ~

Farewell

Willie and Sebastian followed Abigail into the family room, where they found DJ sitting in a new leather recliner with the Davey-sitter beside him and the TV blaring. Sebastian scurried in, jumped into DJ's lap, and then felt the usual gentle pat. There was a faint smile on DJ's face as he held his pet close, slowly stroking Sebastian's fur and calling him Unk.

The moment was interrupted when Abigail said, "DJ, dear, I have something important to tell you."

Abigail pulled up a chair and seated herself directly in front of DJ at eye level. "Honey, you know that Willie and Sebastian...Unk... have been living with us for a while now and—"

A sudden announcement on the TV distracted DJ and he turned away from Abigail.

After turning off the TV Abigail said, "DJ, look at me. Look at my face. Now honey, Unk and Willie need to go back to school."

"Spool."

"School, it's called Enlightenment School."

"Cools."

"No, school."

"Oh."

Sebastian licked DJ on the hand before jumping out of his lap, after which DJ's eyes filled with tears. Abigail leaned over and gave her sad spouse a forehead kiss.

"Willie and Unk promise to visit often, so it's not goodbye. It's only 'so long' for now."

Abigail was surprised when DJ spoke with an emphasis she had not heard for a long time.

"No!"

"I'm sorry, dear, but it needs to be now."

DJ, who had been present for a moment, was again lost in the fog created by his disease. The emphasis in his voice and eye contact with Abigail were replaced by an expressionless face and blank stare. A single tear, leftover from that moment of brief understanding, escaped and trickled down his cheek.

Seeing DJ's tear triggered her own. Abigail didn't want Willie and Sebastian to know how upset she was by their pending departure, so she feigned a sneeze and excused herself to get a tissue.

"Wait for me at the door, I'll be right back."

After drying her eyes and splashing cold water on her face, Abigail met her friends at the back door. "Well, good luck, you two. Be careful and come back often."

Willie responded first. "You know we will, Abbey."

Sebastian followed. "Yeah, we'll see you real soon."

Quickly, and with great anticipation, Willie and Sebastian scooted out the back door.

It was a glorious fall day with a bright blue sky and a warm breeze, a remnant of a summer not ready to be over. Willie and Sebastian scampered around in the dry leaves, stopping here to sniff and there to dig before finding the main entrance to their burrow.

"I forgot how dark it is down here. Abbey's home is always so bright and cheerful."

"Yeah, and I forgot how musty it smells."

They stared into the blackness until their vision adjusted.

"Hey Willie, can you see again?"

"Uh-huh. Look at all those connecting tunnels. There's still a lot to explore, but we better get some rest first."

"And we better figure out what we'll tell our kit coaches when we go back to school."

"Do you think they'll let us back in?"

"Don't know."

It didn't take long for Willie and Sebastian to adjust to their previous nocturnal time clock. For two nights they scrambled to and from the many connecting tunnels, taking time to discuss their return to Enlightenment School.

"Maybe we'll be accepted now that my stripes are coming in and you've lost weight."

"True, and your stripes are growing in, except for your head."

"Whadya mean, except my head?"

"The stripes haven't started to emerge on your head yet."

"Emerge?"

"Oh yes, they're emerging, but I guess the word I meant to say is 'merge.' They're supposed to come together and form a single stripe that goes over your head and down your nose."

"How do you know that?"

"Because I've seen lots of skunks when I was at Enlightenment School."

"What if they don't merge?"

"I'm sure they'll travel the full length of your body. It's probably just a matter of time. Maybe it'll happen once you decide what your second deed should be."

"But what about my skunk-mates? Maybe they'll still make fun of me, call me headless or some other horrible name."

"I won't let them."

"What'll you do?"

"Don't know, but I'll figure something out."

"What should we tell our skunk-mates and kit coaches about where we've been all this time?"

"I think that based on the Three R's, the only responsible thing to do is tell the truth."

"I agree, but how should we tell them?"

"We won't need to tell them."

"Now how do you figure that? If we're going to be truthful, we need to say something, don't we?"

"Not really, we'll simply walk in as if we've never been gone."

"You mean, just appear? All of a sudden?"

"Yup, and then when the questions start, we'll tell the truth. And that way everyone will know."

The next night Willie and Sebastian set off for Enlightenment School.

The evening's early autumn breeze was warm and scented by the recreational burning of fall leaves.

Sebastian and Willie had been traveling for what seemed to them a very long time and stopped to sniff the pungent air.

"Willie, what's that stream down below? I don't recognize it."

"I don't know. Never saw it before."

"I don't remember it being there from when we first went to Enlightenment School. We must have gotten off the path."

"How'd that happen?"

"Guess we were so busy chatting we must have missed a turn somewhere."

"You know, Sebastian, seeing the water makes me really thirsty. Let's go down and get a drink. And then take a swim in the moonlight."

"What about school?"

"We'll never get there in time anyway, because of being lost. And we don't want to be late our first night back, so let's forget about it until tomorrow."

Sebastian was relieved, at least temporarily, as they scurried down to the edge of the stream. Willie was in a hurry to get into the refreshing water.

"Wait, Willie! Don't go in yet." By the time Sebastian said "yet," Willie was already in the water.

"Come on in, Sebastian. It feels great."

"Willie, get out of that water. And whatever you do, don't drink it!"

"Why?"

"I think it's tainted. Get out now! Hurry up."

Begrudgingly, Willie returned to the edge of the stream where he joined Sebastian. "What's wrong?"

"Don't know, but the water smells strange. Almost like skunk stink, but skunks don't let their stink out in water."

"Yeah," Willie sniffed. "Now I smell it. Ugh! Good thing I didn't take a drink."

"Willie, your fur looks greasy."

"Greasy?"

"Slick."

"It's just wet."

"No, it's more than wet. It's matted, too."

Willie licked his fur. "It tastes like the water smells. Oh, what has happened?"

"Listen, Willie, I think there must be something bad in the water."

"I better try to get this stuff out of my fur."

Willie began to roll in a pile of leaves, but things only got worse. The slick residue was like glue, making the leaves stick to his fur.

"Now what am I supposed to do?"

"Willie, there's only one thing we can do."

Simultaneously the two said, "Go back to Abbey."

They hurried back through the woods, and it was dawn by the time they reached the Newton property.

"Look, the Davey-sitter's car is in the drive."

"I can't wait to see Abbey and DJ."

"Me too, but what will she think when she sees the mess I've gotten into this time?"

"She'll help out, just like she did before."

"I know, but she'll be upset about our choices."

"Listen Willie, Abbey said the only way we could learn lessons was through school and experience. Just consider this a bad experience, one we won't make again."

"Well, that's one way to look at it. I guess we better let her know we're back."

Both made their way to the back door, albeit with apprehension.

"You scratch first, Sebastian."

"No, Willie. It's your problem, so you scratch."

Abbey was in the kitchen seated at the island, reading part of a newspaper article out loud to DJ.

"Wait, Willie. Don't scratch yet. I hear Abbey. Let's listen to what she's saying."

They both pricked their ears.

Councilman Dan Guard called for water testing to make sure that nothing is fouling the Penn's Wood water supply. At Mr. Guard's request, council passed a resolution to test water sources for contaminants. Mr. Guard said the contaminants could enter the rivers either through illegal dumping or through municipal wastewater systems. He said he was worried about pollution that could force officials to "put the city on bottled water."

"Willie, did you hear that?"

Willie nodded. "I kind of understood, and it sounds like maybe it has something to do with the bad smell in that stream and whatever made my fur all greasy."

"Yeah, sounds like there could be something wrong with the water. We better get in there and talk to Abbey."

Willie and Sebastian began to squeal loudly and scratch at the door. Shortly thereafter, they were greeted by Abigail,

"Hello, you're back so soon—" Abigail stopped mid-sentence when she noticed Willie's predicament. "For heaven's sake, what on Earth happened to you, Willie?"

"I had an accident, of sorts."

"What kind of accident?" Abigail asked.

"Well, Sebastian and I decided to go back to Enlightenment School, like we talked about, but we got lost on the way."

"Yup, and then Willie saw a stream and decided that, since we were already late for class, we might as well skip classes for the night, get a drink, and enjoy a swim."

"I was so thirsty I rushed in just as Sebastian hollered 'stop'."

"Sebastian, why did you stop Willie?"

"Because the water smelled funny, but Willie was in such a hurry I couldn't stop him in time."

"When I came out of the water, Sebastian said my fur was greasy, so I licked it. And guess what?"

"What, Willie?"

"Well, it tasted bad, like the water smelled."

"How did you get covered in all those leaves?"

"I figured if I rolled in some leaves, they would clean my fur. Instead, all the leaves got stuck all over my body. We didn't know what to do, so here we are."

"Well, you know you're always welcome. I was hoping for a visit, but didn't expect one quite so soon. Sebastian, how about surprising DJ while I clean Willie?"

"That would be wonderful. I missed him so much, and of course I missed you, too."

Abigail prepared a bath of water mixed with detergent. The two chatted while Willie soaked.

"Willie, I need to remind you that part of being responsible is thinking about the consequences of your actions. I think you're still too impulsive."

Willie sighed, head hanging. "You're right, Abbey. You're always right. I'll try to remember." After a moment he continued. "Abbey, I have a question."

"Go ahead. I'll try to answer."

"Before we scratched on the door, Sebastian and I overheard you reading something about the drinking water. Something about it maybe being bad."

"Yes?"

"Do you think it's the same bad thing I found in the stream that got my fur greasy?"

"Probably. Now let's get you out of the tub so I can rub off these leaves."

While Willie was busy with Abbey, Sebastian made himself comfortable in DJ's lap where he was lavished with repetitive stroking. Both Sebastian and DJ were in a deep sleep when Abigail walked in with a now clean Willie at her heels.

Abruptly Willie said, "Wake up, Sebastian. It's time to go."

As had happened a few nights earlier, the three friends gathered at the back door exchanging pleasantries before saying fond farewells.

"Okay, you two, sun's up and you've got to get back to your burrow."

"Yeah, we need to rest before Enlightenment School. And this time, no wrong turns. Okay, Willie?"

"Okay, Sebastian, no wrong turns."

"Bye, Abbey."

"Bye, Sebastian. Bye, Willie. Take care and visit again. I can't wait to hear all about what you learn at school."

Abigail held the door open as Sebastian and Willie scooted out, heading for the backyard burrows, once an annoyance to Abigail but now home to her dear friends.

After a restful day, the kits awoke at dusk, stretched, and shook their fur, readying themselves for the trek to Enlightenment School.

Off they went, grazing on fall berries clinging to thorny bushes, seeds still within open pods awaiting wind travel, and insects caught on the fly. They were about halfway to school when Willie said, "Sebastian, I'm still hungry. I need meat."

"Me too, but if we begin to hunt, we'll be late."

"Yeah, but if I don't get some meat, I'll be too weak to pay attention. There must be something. Maybe a mole or mouse that won't take long to catch."

"Good point, let's look around, and see what we can catch."

Sebastian and Willie had just begun their hunt when they were stopped in their tracks.

"Willie, what's that? That movement? Like the ground's trembling. Do you feel it? There it is again!"

"Oh my stars, for the love of the sun and the moon! I feel it, too. The ground is quivering, but I don't know why."

"Oh, there it goes again," Sebastian cried.

Willie thought for a moment before speaking. "I think the land might be sick, like when we get sick and get the shivers."

"That might be it, but I was shivering after the road striper went over me. Remember that? I wasn't sick then. I was afraid. Maybe the land is afraid."

"That makes sense, too. Either way, the question is why. Why might the land be afraid or why might it be sick?"

"Maybe it's both. Sick and afraid."

"I think we should go back to Abbey."

"No, Willie. We can't keep going back. It's important to figure things out for ourselves."

"Do you think figuring things out has something to do with the Three Rs?"

"I think so, and that's one reason we need to get back to Enlightenment School."

"Oh, no! The ground is shaking again. And it's even stronger this time. I'm scared."

"So am I."

"Listen, Willie, when it stops, let's find something to hold on to."

"Like what?"

"Like a tree branch or a rock. Anything stuck in the ground that won't move."

"Good idea, Sebastian."

Although the Earth's tremble was slight, to Willie and Sebastian and all the other forest animals, insects, and plants, the movement felt enormous, putting the whole forest on alert.

"Willie, it stopped. Hurry, run fast!"

They scurried off the path into the thick of the woods and quickly selected a stout tree in which to find shelter. After climbing a short distance, they found two sturdy branches extending from a thick limb.

"Here Willie, hold on to this branch. I'll hold on to the one right next to you."

They were holding on tight when the trembling began again, this time a little weaker and shorter in duration. Willie and Sebastian thought they were safe, but just after the trembling stopped, they each felt something grab one of their paws.

"Ow! What's that?" Willie cried. "I feel like something's pinching my left paw."

"Something's pinching mine, too, but it's not the left, it's the right."

"Sebastian, what do you think it is?"

"It looks like some kind of weird stick with claws."

"I've never seen anything like a stick with claws."

The strange sticks clamped down even harder, causing the kits to wince. They were trying to shake the sticks off when another round of tremors began. When it was over, the sticks were gone.

"Where'd they go, Willie?"

"There they are, right over there."

"Where?"

"Look up, just above these branches."

"Looks like a couple of twigs to me."

"Well, it's not. It's those strange sticks. I saw them move. Look closer and you'll see their pinchers."

Another brief rumble interrupted their conversation. When they looked up again, the twigs were in a different position and appeared to be praying.

"Willie, say something to them. I think they're alive."

"What should I say?"

"Introduce yourself. Find out who they are and why they're praying."

"Hi, you two ... uh ... sticks. My name is Willie and this is my cousin Sebastian. We were just on our way to school when we felt the Earth shake. We got scared and climbed this tree for protection, but then I think you pinched our paws. You didn't need to do that, because we're friendly-like critters."

The sticks did not respond.

Willie continued his one-sided conversation. "Ever hear of an important stick named Embla? She's very old, but still an expert translator. Maybe you're related."

Suddenly both sticks made hissing sounds.

"I don't know what 'hiss' means."

"It means leave us alone or you're hissstory."

"What?"

"We'll eat you."

"Eat us? You're too small to eat us. We could eat you first."

"Hey, whatever your name is, you and your cousin better look out 'cause we're not the friendly sort."

"Yeah, and we don't know any stick named Embla."

"Furthermore, we may look like sticks but we aren't. That's how we fool you."

"Why do you want to fool us?"

"It's how we get our food. Our meals think we're just another twig or blade of grass, and then—snack attack time. Yum, yum, eat 'um up."

"Ha, Frick, instead of saying snack attack, you could substitute my name. You know, Frack attack. That would really be more like it. Ha ha ha!"

"So Frick and Frack are your names?"

"Obviously. I'm Frick and this is my friend Frack."

"Frick and Frack."

"You got it. But if you're talking to us, you're skating on thin ice."

Willie turned to Sebastian. "Sebastian, what does 'skating on thin ice' mean?"

"Don't know. Ask him."

"Hey Frick, what do you mean by 'thin ice'?"

"I mean, you're taking a chance."

"Why? What kind of chance?"

"The chance that if you get in my way, I'll hurt you bad."

"But how? You don't look so tough."

"You didn't like the pinch I gave your paw, did you?"

"It hurt, but it wasn't that bad."

"That's nothing. I can bite your head off if you get too close."

"What about your friend, Frack?"

"Just as nasty."

"How so?"

"Well now, that's a deep subject. Go ahead, Frack. Tell him all about it.

"Really, Frick, I don't want to discuss the particulars. You know that it wouldn't be good if anything were to leak out. Ha ha!"

"Oh that's rich! Leak out, you say. You're a real blast Frack."

"Frick, hush up."

Sebastian interrupted their conversations. "I don't understand. We saw you praying, and that's a good thing. If you're so bad, why were you praying?"

"Praying?" The sticks burst out hissing. "Now just why would we be praying?"

"Haven't you felt the ground trembling? Aren't you afraid? When I'm afraid, I pray."

"Again, we were fooling you. We pray all right, but there's no prayer involved in the kind of praying we do. We prey for food. Get it? P-R-E-Y, not P-R-A-Y."

"Hmmm, Willie, is there a difference?"

"Must be, but I don't really understand it. To me it sounds the same."

Frick and Frack hissed even louder, "Hiss. You two are just so naive."

"Not too worldly are they, Frick?"

"Entirely gullible, Frack. Maybe we could teach them a thing or two."

"No," Sebastian said. "We already have kit coaches at our school."

"School, huh? Guess you better be on your way before we get hungry cause we frequently devour anything that gets in our way."

Sebastian saw the wisdom in this suggestion. "Willie, let's get away from these greedy strangers."

Sebastian and Willie scampered off the branch and down the tree to the ground below, which was still quivering.

"Willie, we'll never make it to school in time."

"I know, but like I said yester-night, there's always tomorrow."

"Guess we need to go back to Abigail and tell her what's happened."

"Right."

Turning in the opposite direction, they headed for home and arrived at dawn. Just as they had the day before, the two lingered at Abigail's back door, listening in again as she read aloud from the morning paper.

The latest quake, the eleventh since mid-March was the strongest yet. Scientists suspect that some of the injected wastewater migrated into deeper rock formations, allowing an ancient fault to slip...

"Willie, what's a quake?"

"I think it's the sound a duck makes."

"A duck?"

"Yeah, Sebastian, a duck goes quake, quake."

"That doesn't sound right."

"Then I'm not sure."

"What about wastewater?"

"I guess it's water that's wasted."

"But why would anyone want to waste water?"

"I don't know Sebastian. People do strange things."

"Animals don't waste water."

"I know. Humans must be wasteful."

"Okay, Willie, how about the word 'fault'?"

"I've heard Abbey say it's not DJ's fault that he's the way he is."

"But this is an ancient fault."

"Well, we know what ancient means. Our Great[15] Grandfathers lived in ancient times."

"True, but what's an ancient fault?"

"Sebastian, maybe it has to do with the old hamsters on the Isles of Ill."

"How so?"

"Just like Abby said, 'it's not DJ's fault,' and it wasn't the hamsters' fault either."

"You're right. It was the people who took them to the Isles of Ill after they weren't useful as pets anymore. So it was the people's fault."

"Sebastian, good thinking. Maybe what Abbey just read about quakes and faults has to do with people."

"Let's ask her."

Sebastian and Willie began scratching at the door.

When Abbey didn't open the door, the kits began to listen again. What they heard was alarming. Abbey had stopped reading.

The Davey-sitter was screaming, "DJ is having a seizure! I'm calling 911. Hurry, get ready to follow the ambulance when they get here."

"Seizure?" Sebastian said, huddled down by the screen door with Willie. "What's that, Willie?"

"I don't know. Let's listen some more."

They heard the Davey-sitter say, "He's shaking really bad this time, Miss Abbey."

"Willie, maybe DJ has quakes, too."

"Like the Earth?"

"Yup, just like the Earth. Perhaps the Earth has what DJ has."

"You mean Old Hamster's Disease?"

"Uh-huh."

"That's bad, isn't it?"

"Yes, it's bad ... real bad."

Sebastian and Willie remained just outside the back door, ears pricked, tails stiff, and on alert. Within minutes they heard the siren as an ambulance rounded the corner and drove up the Newton's steep driveway.

Oliver began his inevitable barking, prompting Willie to say, "We better get out of here. Abbey has enough trouble already. She doesn't need a visit from us right now."

"Okay, Willie, but I'm worried about DJ and that shaking thing."

"We can watch what happens from our burrow. Just go! Now!"

From the main entrance of their burrow they watched as Abigail opened the door for three paramedics who entered the house, pushing a metal stretcher. After what seemed an eternity, DJ was wheeled out, lying on the stretcher, protected by a blanket and wearing an oxygen mask.

"What's that thing over DJ's mouth and nose?"

"I don't know, Sebastian. I never saw anything like it."

Sebastian and Willie continued their vigil, observing the paramedics cautiously wheel the stretcher into the ambulance and silently drive away with their lights flashing. Then they heard the grind of the garage door as Abigail pulled the car out of the garage.

"Should we follow Abbey?"

"Yeah, let's go."

Unfortunately, the car was already turning onto the street by the time Sebastian and Willie reached the top of the driveway.

Willie turned to Sebastian. "We'll never catch them."

"What should we do?"

"Probably go back to our burrow, get some rest for the day, and then head out for Enlightenment School once it's dusk."

"Willie, I'm so worried about DJ"

"So am I. I'm worried about Abbey, too. But that won't help. We need to do what Abbey wants and that's—"

"Yeah, I know," Sebastian interrupted. "Go to school."

Although Sebastian and Willie tried to rest, there was much squirming and wriggling as the two struggled to process the day's Earth-shattering traumas. At dusk they were still weary. Nonetheless, they understood that the trek to Enlightenment School was inevitable. After a small meal, they set out, this time with greater determination.

"I think I remember how to get there, Sebastian. We just keep following this road."

"Okay, but no getting off course this time."

"Right ..."

Just then a strange looking squirrel crossed their path.

"Sebastian, did you see that?"

"You mean the squirrel?"

"Yes. Have you ever seen a purple squirrel?"

"No, can't say that I have."

"I wonder if it's trying to change its color for some reason."

"Well, it is fall and the leaves change colors, so why not a squirrel?"

"You could be right, Sebastian. Don't forget, according to Dad and Abbey, I'm supposed to change color, too, once its winter."

"And maybe by then my stripes will be complete."

"They will if you find out what your second deed is."

"And that's exactly why we need to get to school. Forget about the squirrel."

"No, I can't. It could be important. Let's just say hello."

"Willie, I don't think—"

Before Sebastian could finish his thought about how this was not a good idea, Willie had already followed the squirrel into the woods. He was introducing himself when Sebastian arrived on the scene.

"Yeah, pleased to meet you, too," the squirrel was saying in a friendly voice. "Tell me your name again."

"It's Willie, and this is my cousin Sebastian. He's a skunk."

"Skunk? But why are his stripes, uh, unfinished?"

Sebastian answered him. "They're coming in. Guess I'm what they call a late bloomer."

"Listen squirrel—" Willie began.

"Name's Spencer."

"Okay, Spencer, how come you're purple?"

"I can't say for sure but my relative told me he thinks it's because I drank water from one of the rivers next to Big City. One day I'm my usual brown squirrel self, and the next thing I know I'm purple. It's strange. The water tasted okay so I kept on drinking. The more I drank, the purpler I got. So, it's gotta be from that river water."

"Where's this river?"

"Like I said, it's one of the rivers by Big City."

"We're woodland animals. We don't know anything about Big City. But, if you're from Big City, what are you doing out here?"

"I came back to live with some relatives. Figure if I drink from the woodland streams, the purple might fade away."

"Well, be careful. We came across a stream right here in the woodlands with some kind of nasty oily substance in it."

"Nasty?"

"Yeah, smelled real bad."

"I saw a couple of raccoons the other night with greasy-like fur, and they were walking real funny, kinda swaying, almost like they didn't know what direction they were going. Kept bumping into each other. And come to think of it, their talk was funny, too. Like they couldn't say their words right."

"Did you ask them what was wrong?"

"No, I thought they might be sick and didn't want to catch anything, so I kept my distance."

"Willie, we better get back on the road to Enlightenment."

"I think we've been on it all along, Sebastian."

"Whadya mean? We got off the road to talk to the squirrel."

"True, and we got off the road several other times, too. But haven't we been learning some important things while we were off the road?"

"Yes."

"So aren't we being enlightened?"

"When you put it that way, I guess I would have to agree."

"Fact is, we need to share what we've learned with our kit coaches."

"Yes, good point. Let's get going."

And off they scampered...on the wrong path in the wrong direction.

~ 12 ~

The Farmer in Dell's Diner

Sebastian and Willie had been traveling for some time on the new path when they came to a clearing in the wood.

"Willie, this open space doesn't look right. I think we went the wrong way. And what's that strange looking house in the distance?"

"Don't know, but the air sure does smell good. I sniff food and I'm really hungry."

"Willie, you did it again."

"Did what?"

"Got us lost. We would have been at Enlighten-ment School by now if you hadn't been distracted by that purple squirrel."

"True, but I think we learned a lot. Remember what I said about enlightenment."

"Yeah, I know, but—"

"No buts. Let's get over there, find some food, and see if there's more to learn."

The two found trash cans filled with scraps of food and partially filled bottles of colas. First they helped themselves to the unfinished hamburgers and cola that had spilled out of an overturned trash can. Willie was the first to hear voices coming from inside the diner where several patrons were engaged in a lively discussion.

Climbing the upright trashcan, Willie balanced himself on the tipsy lid and peered into one of several back windows. "Hey, Sebastian, come on up. This is really interesting."

Sebastian, being his usual cautious self, was hesitant.

"Wow, there are man people sitting on tall seats at a long table and a couple of lady people behind the table giving them stuff to eat and drink. One man person is reading out loud and everyone else is paying attention. What are you waiting for, Sebastian? C'mon up."

Still reluctant, Sebastian joined Willie on top of the trash can.

"Listen to this next article, guys," one of the men said.

> *Something smells in the western neighborhoods of Penn's Wood, and the stench is moving south. "It's skunk," said supervisor Tom Higbee of the Animal Control Division. "We've picked up 42 of the critters so far."*
>
> *Most of the pests have been found in River City, Windward, and Sharpton, but residents living in the southern valley are beginning to report multiple whiffs of pungent skunk spray. According to Higbee, "Some folks have found skunks in traps that were set for raccoons and groundhogs."*

Sebastian was indignant. "Did you hear that about skunks? That's me and my family! Called us pests. I thought I was a pet."

"Yeah, I heard. They picked up forty-two skunks."

"This is terrible. What should we do?"

"Don't know yet, but I'll think of something. Let's keep listening."

...but Higbee has a suspicion. "About two years ago, when we were working in the Western End, a man named Smitty bragged he'd seen hundreds of skunks eating from the troughs of food beneath the Windward Bridge."

Zoologist Dr. Maurice Goffery, an expert on skunks and their habitats, hypothesized that Smitty's explanation is an unlikely cause for the congregating of so many skunks in one particular region. Goffery thinks the animals were drawn to the area by something else which he and his team are now researching. "It's a strange phenomenon and one that I have yet to encounter."

Inside the diner, one of the patrons said "Hey, Higbee, they quoted you."

"Yeah, it's a curious situation, but I gotta do what I gotta do."

"Willie," Sebastian whispered, "what's this guy Higbee 'gotta do'?"

"Don't know yet, but the other guy is reading again. Maybe we'll find out."

Along with his position as supervisor of the Animal Control Division, Higbee owns and operates The Capture Company, which specializes in the capture and relocation of small wild animals. Recently Higbee's company was awarded the contract to deal with the growing skunk problem and has already set traps in over 50 communities.

The Capture Company says it will pick up skunks which have been trapped, but because the Animal Control Division must comply with state regulations, they will be euthanized. Further, Mr. Higbee pointed out that if someone catches a wild animal and releases it into another area, the person could be fined by the Penn's Wood Game Commission.

"Oh, by the blessed memories of our Great[15] Grandfathers! What can this mean?" asked Sebastian.

"I think it means Higbee is going to put out traps, catch as many skunks as he can, and then kill them!"

"Wait, be quiet. They're talking again."

"Hey Higbee, how'd you ever get into the animal business anyway? Doesn't your family own farmland just over the hill?"

"Yeah, Jones. But times are changing. Can't keep up anymore. It just ain't what it used to be. With them factory farms taking over, the little guy can't get a break, and government subsidies are drying up."

"Sounds familiar," Jones said. "My dad sold his land a few years back."

"So who bought your pop's land?" Higbee asked.

"Development company. Cut down all the trees— and I tell ya, they were beauts. Then they built a strip mall. Selling that land was painful, but my pop had no choice. Hurt Ma and Pop real bad.

"Sorry to hear that, Jones. My pap's too old to farm anymore, but he and Maw still live in the old farmhouse."

"So tell me, Higbee. Who tends the crops?"

"The whole family, but we don't make enough money farming to support all of us—them, me and my three brothers, and their families. Everyone works another job and, well, mine is gettin' rid of critters. We scrape by, but times are hard. We'd like to sell, house and land, but the developers stopped building when the housing market dried up, kinda like the land did."

"That's because they over built. Just not enough people for all them houses."

"Yeah, you were lucky to sell when you did, Jones. Now the only thing left to do is lease. See, this land man came callin' and gave me a pitch. Said if I lease my twenty acres, I could get a bunch of money. Seemed like a nice enough fella, really knew his stuff, too. I could sure use that money to fix up the place, but I'm just not sure about this here leasing."

"I know what ya mean. These land men can be slippery. Gotta friend who leased and ended up on the short end of a stick."

"Yeah, what happened?"

"It's secret-like so I can't tell all of it 'cept to say he didn't get enough money to keep paying for water."

"What happened to his well water?"

"Got poisoned and made him and the missus sick. Cows and chickens, too. I feel bad for ya, Higbee. Wouldn't want to make that decision about leasing. Kinda like being between a rock and a hard place, as the saying goes."

"Whadya mean?"

"Listen, some strike it rich and leave town. But others? If you lease, be real careful. Get a good lawyer. The companies stand to make millions. They offer what they call sweet deals, but believe me, if it ain't done right, the deal can turn sour real fast and for lots of reasons."

Throughout the lengthy conversation, Sebastian and Willie sat glued to the trashcan lid with noses pressed to the window. Their only movement was the pricking of their ears, the twitching of their whiskers, and the occasional glance at one another with widened eyes.

"Sebastian, let's get out of here. Forget about Enlightenment School for now. We need to get back to Abbey's and tell her what's going on."

"No, Willie. That would be the worst thing we could do."

"Why? She always has the right answers."

"Because didn't you hear what that man just said? The skunks are moving south and that's where Abbey lives. It's also where that Higbee fellow is setting up his skunk traps."

Sebastian and Willie scrambled down from the trashcans.

"What if I go back to Abbey and you head to Enlightenment School? Once we know more we can meet up again."

"But you need to get to school, too, Willie. And besides, I'm afraid to go by myself."

"Listen, Sebastian, I'm not keen on learning in a school. I'm learning all I need to know right here, out in the open. Like I said before, it's a different kind of learning."

"Well, I guess, but I want to go to Enlightenment School. I want to learn stuff from my kit coach."

"Okay. We just like to learn in different ways, but the main thing is we're both still gonna be taught stuff, just from a different kind of teacher."

"But I've never been alone, Willie. How will I find my way to Enlightenment School?"

"Just keep your nose to the ground and sniff your way. Come on let's get back to the main path."

"Wait! Before we go, let's make a plan to meet up again. We need to share what we learn."

"Right. How about meeting right here, on the next round moon?"

"It's a plan."

~ 13 ~

Sir's Recommendation

Despite some unexpected mishaps along the way, Sebastian reached Enlightenment School and was received by his kit coach and classmates with great delight, especially after they noted his emerging stripes. He had grown in stature and was a handsome skunk with shiny fur and one very white stripe running from tail tip, up over his back, where it stopped abruptly at the juncture of his neck and head. The second stripe had also grown and, although now three quarters of the way up his back, it was not as bright as the first stripe.

On each of the next two full moons Sebastian went back to the meeting place, expecting to see Willie. But Willie never showed up. The first time, Sebastian returned to Enlightenment School feeling downhearted. At the second no show, he returned in a state of panic,

"Sir, I know something bad must've happened to Willie. This isn't like him, not to show up. Where could he be?"

"Most anywhere, Sebastian. Haven't you already learned that weasels are, by nature, most unreliable?"

"I never thought about it, and maybe that's true, but Willie's different. You don't know him like I do."

"Sebastian, eventually you'll catch up with Willie. Perhaps at the next round moon, we can go to your meeting spot together. In fact, I'll ask Coach Politella to join us. We'll make it an outing and surprise Willie."

"How do you know he'll be there if he hasn't shown up so far?"

"I don't. But if he isn't there, we can accompany you to where your friend Abbey lives and try to find out what happened."

"You'd do that?"

"Yes, we certainly would. You've become our prize pupil, and we don't want you to become depressed. We'll help you find Willie."

"Really? Prize pupil? How so?"

"Well, you've learned to direct those bullets in your chamber with greater accuracy than any other kit. At last target practice your score was the highest, hitting the mark ninety-eight percent of the time. You've developed into quite a sharpshooter!"

"I have?"

"Absolutely. In fact, we think you would make an excellent kit coach!"

"I would? Wow!"

"But first you need two more classes, one on battle ethics and one on battle tactics."

"What're they?"

"One is about our moral code. You've learned about the how, now you need to learn about the when, the why, and the where."

"When, why, and where ..."

"Yes, when and when not to use your musk bullets. Why and why not to shoot them. And from where best to shoot. Ethics has to do with the R's of Responsibility and Respect while tactics relates to the R of Resolution."

"I already had a lesson about some of that. It was right before I stopped coming to Enlightenment School."

"You did?"

"Yup, I learned I can't spray a relative, and I can tell you I came really close to breaking that rule."

"When was that?"

"When the kits were mean, ganging up on me all because I was different."

"Yes, it was very unfair. Now that the kits are further along in their development and learning, they've outgrown that silliness. But you need to learn more. That's not the only time shooting our musk bullets is prohibited. It's more complicated than just not shooting your own kind. You need to be able to judge if you are facing an enemy or not. If you do identify an enemy, you need to know when your negotiation skills won't work, leaving you with no alternative but to shoot what's in your arsenal."

"Oh, sounds complicated."

"It is. Strategizing is the key."

"Strata what?"

"Strategizing. It means making a plan."

"What kind of plan?"

"Well, that's all part of the class on tactics."

"When can I start?"

"The sooner the better. It's in our best interest that you advance to the next level as soon as possible. Based on what you've told me about your experiences, along with what you overheard from your friend Abbey and that farmer in Dell's Diner, we may be facing a new and unprecedented enemy."

"Have you figured out what the enemy is?"

"No, but I have an idea and I'll need to tell the other kit coaches."

"Can you tell me?"

"Not yet. First we need to speak with Willie. He may have learned more."

"I hope he shows up at the next round moon."

"This one is called the Cold Moon, Sebastian, and it's soon to arrive. I'll speak with Coach Politella about joining us, but it's almost sun up. Let's get some rest. We'll set out at sundown and tutor you on the way. By the time we meet up with Willie, whether at the meeting place or Abbey's, you'll know all you need to know about ethics and tactics. In fact, you'll need to teach what you learn to Willie."

* * *

The sun was high in the sky. While the kits and coaches at Enlightenment School were fast asleep, Willie, who had adjusted to human patterns, was wide awake, along with everyone else in the Newton household. He was still recuperating from a painful accident that occurred on his way back to Abigail when he was caught in one of the skunk traps laid by Tom Higbee's company. Willie's right paw had finally healed, and the only thing left to do before being cleared by Dr. Murphy to go home to his burrow was remove the bandage.

Because it was so long since he'd seen Sebastian, Willie was overcome with trepidation. Fraught with worry, he wondered if Sebastian had made it back to Enlightenment School. And if so, how had he explained their absence? Was Sebastian angry with him for not showing up at the meeting place twice? What new things had Sebastian learned?

Willie didn't know what trouble he might meet venturing back to Enlightenment School alone. Despite his bravado, his fear was compounded by anxiety over the many traps now scattered throughout the woodlands. Willie didn't want a repeat of what he had just been through. His paw had been mangled, and he was left with a permanent limp.

In the two months Willie had spent with Abigail, he had changed significantly. Like the snow, his fur was now pure white. The day was coming to a close and Abigail wanted to prepare him for the dramatic change he'd undergone.

"Willie, come over here. I want you to see yourself."

Abigail placed Willie on her lap and held up her hand mirror. As he peered at his reflection, Willie was dumbfounded.

"Abigail, I look beautiful."

"Yup, as spectacular as the first snow we had last night. You've transformed from a plain brown weasel into a dazzling white ermine."

"It's astounding. When I was younger and saw my reflection in the woodland ponds, I considered myself plain compared to others in the Mephitidae family. Now, just wait till the kits at Enlightenment School see me."

"Willie, you do know that when summer comes, your fur will again turn brown."

"You mean I'll go back to my other self?"

"Yes, but that doesn't matter. You will always be Willie. What you wear is only a protective covering. The important thing is that your coat keeps you warm."

"That must be what Dad meant when he told me 'One sees clearly only with the heart. Anything essential is invisible to the eyes.' Abbey, I never told you, but the other kits teased me. I used to be stout. And of course you know about Sebastian not having any stripes. The kits were really mean to us."

"Teasing. I know about that, too. And it's a terrible demeaning experience," Abigail agreed. "But before you go, I must warn you. Now that you're a beautiful white ermine, you need to be even more careful in your travels."

"Why? What difference does that make?"

"It's dangerous because of the trappers, hunters who set steel devices with claws that catch animals."

"You mean the kind I already got caught in?"

"Yes, exactly."

"Why would a hunter want to catch me, a measly weasel? We heard they're trapping skunks."

"People want for themselves what you have naturally. And besides, you are not measly, Willie."

"But I still don't get it."

"This is tough to explain, but I'll try. The trappers kill animals, skin them, and then sell the skins, also called pelts, to people who sew them together to make clothing—mainly hats, coats, shrugs, or even purses or belts. People who live in winter climates buy and wear your fur for two reasons. First to keep them warm. And second because ermine fur makes them look important."

"But I don't feel important because of my ermine fur. Why would they?"

"Ermine is one of the most expensive furs, even more expensive than mink."

"They kill minks, too?" Willie squeaked. "Abbey do you have any fur clothes?"

"No, I'm an animal lover, so I would never buy anything made out of fur, but some people are vain."

"Vain?"

"Yes, they don't see with their hearts. Instead they admire the wrong things, like animal furs, expensive animal furs like yours."

* * *

"Are you ready, Sebastian?"

"Yup, all set, Sir."

"Then let's pick up Coach Politella and get going."

The December's full moon was at its brightest, lighting the way, first to the meeting place, where Willie was again a no show, and then to Abigail's. The kit coaches schooled Sebastian throughout the journey on ethical and tactical decision making. They were making good progress until the woods began to thin with the emergence of a few people houses. It was then they noticed the animal traps, at least one in each of the people back yards.

When the woods gave way to whole neighborhood developments, the number of traps grew proportionately, and their progress was slowed considerably. As they picked their way through, Sebastian reminded

Sir and Coach Politella about the newspaper article describing a mysterious increase of skunks and the plan to exterminate his kindred.

"It's that Higbee fellow, the one Willie and I overheard."

"Why, that's an outrage. How dare humans consider us pests. The nerve!"

"Exactly my thoughts, Sir. If only they understood how important we are to the environment. And not only that, but skunks can be pets. I'm DJ's pet, not his pest."

"Amazing how one small squiggle can completely change the meaning of a word."

"Yeah—I mean yes—Sir."

As Sebastian, Sir, and Coach Politella neared the people backyards, they were unprepared for what they heard, smelled, and saw. First was the high-pitched screeching of trapped skunks, communicating fear, anguish, pain, and untold suffering. Then the stench of skunk feces and urine began to burn their nostrils. If that wasn't horrific enough, there was the appearance of the skunks themselves: dirty, disheveled, and noticeably distraught.

It was the forlorn expression in the eyes of one particular skunk however, that stung Sebastian most. She was alone, shivering in a bent, rusty cage. Although she wasn't screeching like the others, her soft whimper seemed louder to Sebastian than any of the other cries for help. Sebastian could see that she was especially beautiful, despite the enforced captivity. Her stripes were broader than most, creating a deeper cleavage at the point of her head, and her scent was ... well suffice it to say that the attraction was instant. Sir and Coach Politella noted Sebastian's distraction.

"Sebastian, snap out of it. We need to do something about this and fast."

"Yes, yes, of course we must. This is worse than I imagined. Listen, that cage over there, the one that caught my attention, is in Abigail's backyard, near Willie's and my burrow. That means we're finally here."

"That's great news and it's perfect timing, because it's almost sun up."

Coach Politella said, "Sir, I say we get some grub and settle down in Sebastian's burrow. Then after a few sun ups we'll be rested and ready to make a plan."

"My feelings exactly, Politella. Okay, Sebastian, lead the way."

The three settled in for the day just as Abigail returned from Dr. Murphy's office, where Willie's bandages had been removed. She knew it was time to say goodbye yet again, and was concerned about Willie's safety.

When Abigail pulled into the garage, she experienced a mixture of strange sensations—a sudden chill causing goose bumps on her arms, followed by an unexplained exhilaration and nervousness. Then Willie became agitated, scraping at the bars of the cage and jumping up and down, squealing with delight. They both sensed Sebastian's proximity.

"Willie, it's Sebastian, isn't it?"

Willie could hardly contain himself. Abigail opened the car door and released Willie. He leaped out, running straight for the backyard burrow as well as he could, given his limp.

Abigail shouted, "The traps! Be careful—" but her warning went unheard as Willie safely slipped down the burrow's main entrance.

What a joyous reunion it was! Sir and Coach Politella looked on as Willie and Sebastian embraced, tears seeping from their eyes and matting the fur underneath.

"Is it really you, Willie? You've changed so much."

"Yup, I'm not a measly weasely anymore."

"So what are you?"

"Abbey said I'm an ermine."

"Ermine?"

"Yup, remember? It's what all weasels become in the winter—like the snow."

"You look beautiful."

"Yeah, for now, but I'll change back to the other me in the spring."

"I don't care. I love you no matter what, and I'm glad we're back together."

"Sebastian, you look different, too. Your first stripe is complete and your second stripe has grown. Did you find out what your second deed is supposed to be?"

"Not yet, but the stripe has grown anyway, and I don't know why. It's a mystery."

Sebastian and Willie talked well into the dwindling light of day. Instead of resting, Sebastian told Willie what Sir taught him about ethics and tactics. Willie told Sebastian about being caught in one of the skunk traps. They discussed the plight of the captured skunks and what could be done. Sebastian even told Willie about that one special skunk that had distracted him.

Without disturbing the kits, Sir and Coach Politella listened to their conversation. Finally, when Sebastian and Willie were all talked out and the kit coaches were all listened out, all four had come to a single conclusion. The skunks needed to be saved. The question was, how?

~ 14 ~

Beauregard

Addressing Sebastian and Willie, Sir said, "Kits, we've been in your burrow for two sunrises and one moon set. It's time Coach Politella and I get back to Enlightenment School."

Politella followed with, "Sir's right. We're planning to leave at sundown tomorrow. The two of you pretty much know what you're supposed to do."

"Let's review the plan thus far," Sir continued. "Willie, you go first."

"Okay, here goes. I trip the traps, free the skunks, and bring the hostages to our burrow."

"Correct," said Coach Politella.

Sir asked, "Sebastian, what happens next?"

"Every evening I greet the skunks, give them food and water, and make sure they rest up. I do this until all the skunks are free, so it'll take several evenings. After that, Willie and I lead the skunks to Enlightenment School, where we'll meet up with you and Coach Politella. Right?"

"Yes, but there's more to it than that."

"More?" Willie asked.

"Politella, go ahead and explain what happened yesterday."

With deference, Politella responded, "No, I'll let you do the honors, Sir, since you met him first."

Sebastian and Willie chimed in. "Met who?"

"Beauregard."

"Beauregard? Who's that?"

"He's a groundhog. An important groundhog. A groundhog extraordinaire!"

"Sir, I couldn't have said it better myself."

"Why thank you, Politella."

"Kits, Beauregard will play a critical role in transporting the two of you and all the skunks back to the school."

Sebastian and Willie peppered Sir with questions.

"How did you meet this groundhog?"

"How long have you known him?"

"Can he be trusted?"

"What makes him so important?"

Sir interrupted, "Whoa now, give me a chance. I'll explain, but it's a long story."

"Okay, but please hurry up. I can't stand waiting!"

"Willie, you must learn to be patient," Sir said shaking his head.

Willie took a deep breath and exhaled with a sigh. "I'll try."

"Now, are you both ready to listen? Last eve, Coach Politella and I became curious about the many tunnels throughout your burrow and decided to have a look around while you were napping. During our exploration, we stumbled upon a long, winding underground passage that ended in a T where two perpendicular extensions branched out going north and south. Off these extensions were other branches going east and west. We decided to travel along the southerly extension. I was in the lead when we heard digging ahead, as if someone or something was shoveling dirt. The farther south we went, the louder the noise became. Finally, I found myself staring at the hind end of a land beaver."

"Land beaver?" Sebastian asked, perplexed. "Willie, you ever hear of a land beaver?"

"No, can't say that I have."

"So tell us, Sir," Sebastian asked again, "What kind of animal is a land beaver?"

"A land beaver is a woodchuck. In some places they're called whistle pigs. But, in all cases, no matter what the name, it means the same thing, and that's groundhog. Beauregard is the largest groundhog we've ever seen. And he's a general, General Beauregard Lee."

"General of what?"

Sir answered definitively, "He's the general of an underground movement."

"Underground movement?"

"Willie, you've got to stop interrupting. You'll understand when I finish the whole story."

"Sorry, Sir."

"So, as I was explaining, Coach Politella and I found ourselves staring at the hind end of a huge groundhog. I cleared my voice so as not to startle him and when he turned around, I excused myself for interrupting his dig. At first he was surprised to see us but collected himself and said, 'Well, howdy-do, y'all, allow me to introduce mahself. I am General Beauregard Lee, but you can call me

Beauregard.' He spoke funny, kind of drawling out his words. Told us it's a Southern accent."

Sebastian asked, "What's a Southern accent?"

"Beauregard's from a place called Peachtown, way down south of here, and that's how they talk, kind of lazy-like. Then he told us that none of the groundhogs saw their shadows this year, so he called a groundhog convention up north of us. Then he said he was digging his way home because of all the traps above ground. And then he made a joke saying, 'From now on, we groundhogs will use the tunnels to travel distances. You could say we've purt near gone and 'stablished an underground movement.' So there you have it.'

"Wow!" said Sebastian.

Sir continued, "I asked Beauregard what it means if a groundhog doesn't see his shadow. He said there would be an early spring. Then I asked him if that was unusual and why none of the other groundhogs saw theirs. He said, 'You bet it's unusual. All the groundhogs agree—something's happening to the Earth. Even heard tell that polar bears are suffering because their homes are melting'."

This time, Willie interrupted. "That's terrible, but please tell us how this Beauregard is going to help the skunks."

"I'm getting to that part. Beauregard, like all groundhogs, is a natural engineer, just like the beavers except that groundhogs build underground tunnels and beavers build dams. I told him how we need to get back to school and about the skunks caught in traps. But when I told him our plan, he said, 'If'n y'all travel above ground, it'll be real dangerous.

144

Lemmie help ya git there using our underground. Jus' point me in the direction of this here school and I'll dig y'all there.' That's what he said and now you know why I said Beauregard's the leader of an underground movement."

Willie said, "Oh, now I get it."

Coach Politella finally got a word in. "Since Beauregard is already digging south, and Enlightenment School is on his way, he'll gladly help us."

Willie interjected, "Us? Do you mean you 'us' or me and Sebastian 'us'?

"I mean Coach Politella and myself."

"That means he'll help you and Sir. But if the two of you leave with Beauregard and we stay here, how will we meet up with you? And don't forget, our plan also includes me and Sebastian visiting Abbey to find out if she knows what's going on in Penn's Wood. You know, about the water, the ground shaking, and what's happening to the farmers' land. Maybe there's a connection between what we experienced and what the groundhogs learned when they didn't see their shadows. It all seems to do with the Earth."

Sebastian added, "Sounds to us like the Earth might be sick, like DJ. And if that's true, we'll all be sick. We need to find out."

"Very astute observations," Coach Politella said. "Sir and I agree with both of you. Obviously something's not right, and since animals are closer to the ground than humans, they figure things out faster than humans. Eons ago animals and humans shared the Earth's space and depended on each other for survival. Back then humans were in tune with nature and the nuances of animal language. But now, even though humans may have pets and can learn from some of their habits, the lessons are mostly indirect. The original link between animals and humans has been lost, so the animals may have to help humans in a direct manner now. But we'll get to that part after you both return to Enlightenment School."

"Yeah, but how are we—me, Sebastian and the rest of the skunks—supposed to get back if you and Sir leave with Beauregard?"

Sir provided the answer. "Here's how it'll work. Beauregard said he'll backtrack and get you and the other skunks after he's finished digging me and Politella to school."

"Oh, that makes sense," said Willie. "It'll give me time to round up the skunks. It'll give Sebastian time to give them food and water. And it'll give the skunks time to rest up before their journey."

General Beauregard arrived the following dusk, and Coach Politella introduced him to Sebastian and Willie. At first, the kits were intimidated by Beauregard's sheer size, but after the enormous groundhog began to speak, they were put at ease by his jovial manner.

"So y'all are the kits! Well, howdy-do and pleased ta make your acquaintance. Mistuh Sir and Mistuh Politella here tol' me all 'bout you young'ns. Now see here,"— General Beauregard pointed to Sebastian —"Skunk, what's your name, again?"

In a small voice, Sebastian answered.

"Well, Sebastian, I see ya got one full stripe and another coming along right nice. From what Sir tells me, looks like you'll have that in no time. Yup, no time a'tall."

Then he pointed to Willie, "And you're Willie, right?"

"Yup, that's me, I'm a weasel— I mean, ermine."

"Well, Skunk Sebastian and Ermine Willie, it's time for us to depart."

The kits and their coaches excused themselves for a private goodbye. Bowing their heads in unison, each gently tapped one another's head, a sign of good luck and good fortune. Then Sir and Coach Politella left with Beauregard, for an interesting and most educational dig. When they were no longer in sight, Sebastian scrambled out of the burrow's main entrance, hurrying to get to the Newton house with Willie following, slowed by his limp. Each knew this would be a perfect place to begin their sleuthing, before all the other activities got underway.

~ 15 ~

The Plot Thickens

Sebastian was excited to see Abigail and even more so his pal DJ, as it had been a long time. After scurrying across the yard, he reached the backdoor and then waited for Willie before scratching on the door.

When Abigail answered the door and saw her animal friends, she was thrilled. "Sebastian! Willie! You're here and together again. Seeing the two of you back together is the best thing that's happened to me in a long time. Come on in. We can chat in the family room."

"Yum, something smells good."

"It's a pot of chicken soup. I was just thickening it."

"Thickening the soup?"

"Yes, for DJ. He's having trouble swallowing, and it's easier for him if I thicken the soup."

"How do you do that?"

"I take the noodles out, mash them up, put them back in the soup, and then stir it all together."

"Does it taste good that way?"

"It's okay. I prefer it thin, but DJ doesn't cough or choke when I thicken it."

Alarmed, Sebastian asked, "Whadya mean, choke?"

Abigail's expression changed, and both animals could feel the pain in her heart and hear the catch in her throat when she started to speak.

"He's failing," Abigail answered, with lips quivering and eyes beginning to redden.

"Failing, how?" Sebastian asked.

"He's sleeping more, eating less, losing weight, and coughing or choking when he eats. Worst of all, he's having more seizures."

"Seizure? What's that?" Willie asked.

"It's a kind of shaking."

"Like when he's cold?" Sebastian suggested.

"No, it's much worse than just being cold. His whole body jerks and shakes."

Sebastian's whiskers began to twitch. "Abbey, that sounds scary."

"It's worse than scary, because there's more that happens when he has one of those seizures."

Both Willie and Sebastian grew quiet, giving each other a worried glance.

Willie broke the momentary silence. "More than scary? Abbey, tell us the rest."

"Okay, but the rest is really frightening. DJ's eyes roll back in his head, and his breathing becomes very heavy and noisy. Afterward, he's stiff and doesn't move. About a month ago, when he could still stand and walk—"

"What?" Sebastian interrupted. "Can't DJ walk anymore?"

"I was just about to explain. DJ had a bad seizure in the middle of the night when he tried to get out of bed. That's when he fell and hit his head. There was a bad gash on his forehead. He was bleeding and needed stitches, so the Davey-sitter called an ambulance. I followed the ambulance to the emergency room and after DJ was admitted, I stayed with him for what the rest of the night and the next day."

Sebastian turned to Willie, "That must have been what we saw that night."

"Oh yes, of course," Willie replied. "Abbey, you didn't answer the door, and we hurried back to our burrow."

"Yeah, then we hid out and watched," Sebastian chimed in. "We even tried to follow you."

"Follow me?"

"Yes, you were following the...the ambulance. That's what you just called it."

Abbey was astounded, "You watched? I didn't even know you were there. Why were you at the door?"

"Well, we felt the Earth shaking a whole lot so we climbed a tree. And after the Earth stopped shaking, we were so scared we came back to you instead of going to school. But enough about that. Tell us what happened to DJ."

Abigail frowned. "Well, after he came home from the hospital, it seemed like he couldn't remember how to put one foot in front of another."

Sebastian asked again, "So that's when he stopped walking?"

"Yes. It's what Alzheimer's disease does. People grow backward from adulthood to childhood, and from there, back to infancy. But they stay physically big, and that makes it hard to take care of them."

Abigail could not contain herself and began weeping.

Sebastian crawled into Abbey's lap. "What will happen next? Will DJ get worse?"

Sniffling, Abigail answered, "Yes, he's like a sinking ship."

"Sinking ship? Oh, no! Willie, remember how one of the Isles of Ill sank after the hamsters with Old Hamster's disease hardened?"

"Yes, the island got too heavy to float." Willie looked down at his paws.

Sebastian said, "Abbey, do you think this isle will sink the same as DJ?"

"What isle do you mean?"

"I'm talking about our place, where we all live. Do you think that if enough people get Old Hamster's Disease our place will harden and sink?"

"Hmmm. Never thought of it that way, but there *are* some bad things happening in Penn's Wood."

Sebastian changed the subject, sure he could get more information from Abigail when she was less upset. "May I go see DJ now?"

"Sure, he's in bed, but don't be surprised if he doesn't seem to know you."

"I'll crawl into his arms. I bet he'll know it's me,"

"I just don't want you to be disappointed if he doesn't."

After Sebastian left the room, Willie explained how the kit coaches had accompanied Sebastian to her home and about the many traps they had seen along the way. Willie was in the middle of describing the awful condition of the trapped skunks when Sebastian returned, looking sad and downhearted.

"You weren't gone very long. What happened?"

"Well, I jumped into DJ's lap like I used to, but he never reached down to pet me. Not even once. I cuddled up to him and even brushed my tail across his arm, but he didn't move. Never even opened his eyes."

Abigail gently stroked Sebastian. "Yes, I understand how hard that must be for you, because it makes me feel the same way when I give him a kiss or a hug, or pat his head."

"Oh, Abbey, it's terrible!"

"I know but there's nothing we can do. Once the disease starts, you can't stop it. I used to feel hopeful but now I just feel helpless."

Willie broke the tension. "Listen Abbey, I have an idea."

"What is it, Willie?"

"I know you can't help DJ anymore, but maybe you can do some other good thing."

"Like what?"

"Like, help me and Sebastian save the trapped skunks."

Then Abigail said, "Yes, we were just talking about that. Finish telling me about these trapped skunks, Willie."

"Okay, well the skunks are being trapped by this man, what's his name again, Sebastian?"

"Tom Higbee."

"Yes, that's him. Once he's done trapping the skunks he's going to kill them."

Abigail scratched her head and said, "Yes, there was an article about it in the newspaper a while back. It's a nasty business. But how do you two know about this?"

Willie was the first to respond. "Me and Sebastian kind of met Tom Higbee."

"What do you mean, you met him?"

"It was when we were on our way to school and got off the path again and—"

"It was your idea to get off the path," Sebastian interrupted.

"Yeah, I admit it. It was my fault. But I saw this purple squirrel and we never saw a purple squirrel before and—"

"You didn't have to follow him into the woods," said Sebastian.

"But Sebastian, I thought Spencer—that was his name —would give us some information. I thought his purple fur was a clue to what's going on."

"Well it didn't really help, and when we tried to get back on the path, that's when we got lost."

Abbey asked again, "How did you meet Tom Higbee?"

Willie said, "So here we were on this wrong path when I smelled food. And of course it made me hungry. Anyway there was this place and we peeked through a window. And that's when we heard these two people who said they were...uh, what were they, Sebastian?"

"Farmers, but I don't know what that is. One was named Jones and the other was this Higbee guy."

Abigail was amazed. "What were they talking about?"

Willie turned to Sebastian, "Didn't Higbee say he needed more money and that's why he became an exterminator?"

"Yes, and he said something else, too. It was about his farm."

"That's right. Now I remember. He said life was hard and he was trying to sell his land, even though he didn't want to, but no one was buying farmland anymore."

"And he also said something about maybe leasing his land, Willie. Whatever that is. Then that other guy, Jones, told him to be careful and get a lawyer. We didn't hear any more because we left after that."

Sebastian picked up the conversation. "There's something else, Abbey. It might even be related to why the skunks are being trapped and killed."

"What's that, Sebastian?"

"Me, Willie, and the kit coaches think something bad might be happening to the land."

"Okay, but what does that have to do with the skunks being trapped?" Abigail asked.

"It was in that newspaper article. It said lots of skunks are moving to South Penn's Wood, and they don't know why."

"Yes, that's true. The article did say that," Abigail confirmed

"Well, we have a hunch."

"Okay, what do you and Willie think?"

"We think the humans are doing something in this part of Penn's Wood that's causing the skunks to gather."

Abigail asked, "But gather for what purpose?"

154

"We don't know that yet," Sebastian said. "Sometimes when animals sense danger, they either move away from it or toward it."

"Toward it? Why move toward danger?" Abigail asked.

Sebastian's response was right to the point. "To fight!"

Willie looked agitated. All the talk was making him nervous. And when he was nervous, he got hungry. "Let's take a break and have a snack."

So the three went into the kitchen and gobbled down a couple of peanut butter sandwiches before resuming their discussion.

"Abbey, do you remember when Willie got that smelly grease on him after going for a swim in one of the woodland ponds?"

"How could I forget? He was a mess."

"Do you think that the water was poisoned?"

"Yes, Sebastian, I definitely think it was polluted, or poisoned, as you said."

"Abbey, do you know what's polluting the water?"

Abbey wrinkled her forehead. "I think so, but you're asking some very tough questions."

Sebastian continued, "Yeah, Abbey, you said something bad is happening in Penn's Wood."

"I did say that but let's not talk about it now. I want to know more about how we can free the skunks."

Willie's ears began to prick and his whiskers twitched, "That's my job. And like I said, Abbey, you can help. Here's the plan. Each sundown I'll travel around the back of the people houses. Wherever I find trapped skunks, I'll open the locking bar and free them. They'll follow me to our burrow where Sebastian will feed them. Then when all the skunks have been gathered, we'll take them with us to Enlightenment School where we'll meet with our kit coaches."

"Where do I come in?" Abbey asked.

"Sebastian needs help gathering enough food for so many skunks. Your job will be to bring berries and other stuff to our burrow. Will you help us, Abbey?"

"Absolutely. I'll get started first thing in the morning. But I'm wondering how you'll get back to school safely since Higbee and his crew are still busy laying traps all over the area."

After Sebastian and Willie explained the plan to Abigail, including all about General Beauregard, she invited them to stay at her place for the night rather than return to their burrow.

"You know, kits, I'm really tired, and we all have a big day ahead. Let's call it a night. In the morning I can begin gathering food, and you can return to your burrow."

Abigail paused and then added, "And I have a favor to ask."

"What is it?" Sebastian questioned.

"Never mind, I'll save it for tomorrow. Right now I'm heading upstairs to bed. Time to sink into my soft pillows."

After Abigail left, Sebastian asked Willie, "What favor do you think Abbey wants?"

"Don't know. Maybe it has to do with DJ. Anyway, we're all tired. She'll tell us tomorrow."

Upstairs Abigail intended to sleep away her worries, worries that included DJ's decline, her resolve to assist the skunks, her suspicions about what was happening in Penn's Wood, and the favor she needed to ask Sebastian and Willie.

Like Abigail, Sebastian and Willie were exhausted. They too had experienced a multiplicity of strong emotions including excitement fostered by their reunion with Abigail, apprehension over what was happening to the environment, anticipation regarding freeing the skunks, sadness over DJ, and curiosity about Abigail's unasked question. The kits were drained, and the only thing left to do was say a simple goodnight before curling up and falling asleep.

During the night, the weather changed dramatically, going from rain to sleet, sleet to snow, and finally, just before dawn, a full blizzard, complete with howling winds.

~ 16 ~

Aunt Agram's Visit

"Willie, wake up. You're talking in your sleep."

"What?"

"Wake up!" Sebastian nudged Willie until he opened his eyes and began to stir.

He started mumbling to Sebastian, "Let me be, it's not time to get up yet."

"Yes it is. It's daylight."

"But, I don't hear Abbey making morning noises, and the house is still quiet. I don't even hear DJ or the Davey-sitter."

"He's not here yet, but you still need to get up."

Just after Willie mentioned the Davey-sitter, the garage door began to creak and rumble. Oliver bounded out of his crate and started barking at the basement door.

The Davey-sitter let himself in from the garage to the basement. He took off his wet winter outerwear and hung it on a hook. Then he took off his boots and placed them on the floor mat. The sitter climbed the steps to the first floor and upon entering the kitchen was greeted by all three household pets. Although he didn't have Abigail's gift of animal telepathy, he began to engage in a one-sided conversation with the animals.

"Good morning. Last night's snow was a heavy one, so we'll be shut-ins today. There's even a story about the storm in this morning's newspaper." The Davey-sitter flung the paper onto the small corner desk.

"Couldn't even get my car up the driveway. Had to walk up. Good thing my new boots have deep treads or I'd still be at the bottom of the drive, along with the car."

Oliver began sniffing the Davey-sitter's feet. Willie and Sebastian just looked on and, as usual, avoided contact with the dog. Once satisfied that he had properly greeted the sitter, Oliver moseyed over to the corner farthest from Willie and Sebastian and began licking his empty bowl.

"Wanna eat before I wake up DJ?" The dog's action prompted the sitter to prepare breakfast for the pets.

All three animals pricked their ears, looking attentive while the sitter opened a can of wet dog food and spooned it into Oliver's bowl. Then he scooped out dry pellets for Willie and Sebastian.

"Okay, now that you have a good breakfast, I'm going to check on DJ."

Oliver wasn't that hungry and after eating only part of his breakfast meal, wandered off for unknown parts leaving Willie and Sebastian alone.

"Willie, you were mumbling some really weird things in your sleep this morning."

Willie asked, "Oh yeah? What'd I say?"

"Well, it sounded like you were having a conversation with an aunt somebody or other. I couldn't quite make out her name"

Willie wrinkled his brow. "Hmmm ... I hardly ever dream. Try to remember. Maybe it's important."

Sebastian thought about it. "It sounded something like the word program or telegram."

Willie said, "Now I remember! My Great[15] Grandfather's Aunt Agram visited me last night."

"Willie, that's impossible. Your Great[15] Grand Aunt Agram has been dead for eons."

"No, Sebastian, I don't mean for real. She came to me in a dream during last night's storm." Willie thought for a moment. "Or was that part of my dream? I'm not sure now. Did you hear the wind howling?"

"Nope, I slept all night. But according to the Davey-sitter, there must have been a very big storm."

Willie continued. "In my dream I saw my aunt float into the room right through the window, even though it was closed tight. Very strange."

"What did she look like?"

"Well, her fur was winter white and thinning at the top. Her eyes were small but intense. She looked a little shriveled and very old."

"Did she say anything?"

"Yes, come to think of it, she did. And you won't believe what she said."

"Okay, okay, tell me what she said."

"She said—now get this—that I must help you finish earning your second stripe."

"Wow! Did she tell you what I'm supposed to do?"

Willie put a paw to his brow, deep in thought. "Hmmm, it's hard to remember but I think it had to do with helping Abbey."

"So your old Aunt Agram told you to help me help Abbey with something?" Sebastian was getting frustrated. "Willie, try harder. What was the something I'm supposed to help Abbey with?"

"With ... with ... Oh! I remember now. You're supposed to help Abbey stop whatever bad might be happening in Penn's Wood."

"But Willie, how can you help me help Abbey when you don't even know exactly what's happening? And neither do I."

Willie's eyes grew wide. "Sebastian, Abbey must know. She's given hints, and eventually she'll tell us. Listen, there must be a way for me to help you to help Abbey or my aunt's spirit wouldn't have visited me and said what she said. Give me a minute to think... Remember in *Die Alten Tage* when my Great[15] Grandfather Mordecai used Aunt Agram's problem solving method to figure out a way for the skunks to escape from their homeland?"

"Sort of. I remember they used a raft."

"That's right, but do you remember how he thought up the raft idea in the first place?"

"No. I was getting sleepy when Mom was reading that part, but I think your aunt taught your grandfather to use some kind of word game."

"Exactly! She taught him to take the last sentence of an important conversation and rearrange the letters of each word until a solution was revealed."

"I forget. What word did your Great[15] Grandfather finally use to give him his raft idea?"

"It was fart, Sebastian ... F-A-R-T."

"Oh yes, how could I have forgotten?"

"Sebastian, do you remember our last conversation with Abbey?"

"Sure, she told us she needed a favor then she said she was tired. After that she went upstairs."

"Yes but she said something else. What was it? Something about her pillows."

"You're right! She did mention soft pillows. I think she said 'sink into soft pillows'."

"Yup, that was it! I'm sure of it. Now which of the words should I try to rearrange ... sink, soft, or pillows? Those were the main words. I'll try pillows first, it's the longest. Let's see, where can I write the letters?"

Instinctively Willie began looking around for something to dip his paws into. He wandered over to Oliver's dog bowl where the unfinished breakfast remained mushy in the bowl.

"Here, come on over. I can use the leftovers in Oliver's bowl. And guess what, I can eliminate the word 'pillows' right away because it's too many letters to fit in the bowl. So that leaves 'soft' and 'sink'. I'll try 'soft' first."

Willie began rearranging the letters. "F-T-O-S ... Nope. T-O-S-F ... Nope. O-T-S-F ... Nope. Soft is not the word. Let me try 'sink.' It's the only one left."

"Go ahead, Willie. Try it."

"Okay, here goes. I-N-K-S ... it's a word but not the right word. K-I-N-S ... it's a word, too, but doesn't ring any bells. S-K-I-N. Now there's a word. But nothing comes to mind with that one, either.

"Listen, Willie, maybe 'sink' is the word. You know, all by itself, without being rearranged. Give it some time and you'll figure it out. You have to!"

Sounding discouraged Willie said, "Okay, I hope I'll come up with something soon." Then with pricked ears he said, "But we better stop talking. I hear Abbey's footsteps. She's coming downstairs."

Still groggy from her night of tossing and turning, Abbey padded into the kitchen and over to the coffee pot, thankful for its preprogramming function that automatically ground and brewed her usual two cups.

As she poured, she greeted the kits, albeit not too enthusiastically. "G'morning. You guys get any sleep last night?"

Sebastian and Willie glanced at one another and made a few positive animal noises, indicating they had slept well.

Abbey said, "Not me. I hardly got a minute's rest. Weird dreams kept interrupting me all night long."

Willie said, "I had a dream, too. It was about —"

"Hold on a minute, Willie!" Abbey was suddenly distracted when she heard the phrase "explosion reported" coming from the countertop TV that the Davey-sitter habitually kept on all day. "The news just came on and I want to listen," she said as she turned up the volume.

At 6:15 this morning, one of three tanks near the Augustus Shale wellheads caught fire. It has been reported that the compressor station at the well site exploded. Initial findings suggest that the explosion occurred due to a malfunctioning heater, causing the hatch of a second tank to blow off, catching fire. Three workers were injured and are currently being treated for second degree burns. It's unclear at this time if residents living within the area need to be evacuated. As more information is available, we will keep you posted. This is Amy Gold, reporting live on location.

Abigail took a deep breath, sighed, and began a tightlipped, angry mumble. "So there you have it. Today an explosion, yesterday dumping, and the day before that, leakage. It just keeps getting worse. Who knows what tomorrow will bring."

This was it, the chance Sebastian and Willie had been waiting for. They eyed each other and Willie nudged Sebastian. "I told you Abbey knows what's going on."

Then Willie turned to Abbey. "Uh, Abbey, there's something we've been wanting to talk to you about."

"Okay. Go ahead, I'm listening."

"Abbey, is this—I mean what you just said—is this the bad stuff that's happening in Penn's Wood?" Willie asked.

Sebastian followed with, "Do you think it's why DJ's sick?"

Willie jumped back in. "Does it have to do with what we found on the way to Enlightenment School, and the reason our kit coaches are worried?"

Next Sebastian interrupted. "And the reason the animals are behaving in strange ways?"

Their questions came so fast that Abigail didn't have a chance to answer. Finally, out of breath, the excited kits took a break. This pause gave Abigail a chance to respond.

In a hushed voice she said, "Yes, yes, yes ... and yes."

"But Abbey, what's the cause?"

"The best answer I can give you is this: just like people and animals need food to live, things need food, too, to make them go."

Willie asked, "Like what kinds of things and what kinds of food?"

Abigail pointed. "Well, like ... okay, see my refrigerator? It needs a food called electricity to keep stuff cold. And my car. You've seen me fill it up with gas. That's the kind of food a car uses to make it move."

"So is this all about getting food for your things so they come to life?" Sebastian asked.

Abigail answered with a simple, "Yes," and then added, "So things can operate."

"But Abbey, why would that harm the Earth?"

"Because ..." She paused to think, finding it difficult to explain an intricately complex situation in a simple way, a way her animal friends would be able to understand.

"Let's just say most of the food or energy needed by things is being dug out from deep underground. Since more and more people have more and more things, we're running out of this kind of food, or energy."

Sebastian grew excited. "Willie, remember when our Great[15] Grandfathers almost ran out of food during their adventure in the olden days?"

"Sure, they found another food source."

"What was it?" Abigail asked.

Sebastian said, "Plants from the bottom of the sea."

"Well, animals are smart," Abigail said. "We humans also have other ways to get food and energy for our things, but we don't like change."

"But Abbey, me and Sebastian still don't know why bad things are happening in Penn's Wood."

"Well, kits, instead of changing to a different food source for our things, people have discovered a new way to keep getting more of the old type of food out from under the ground. And it's this new method that's causing explosions, earthquakes, water pollution, and sickness in Penn's Wood."

"What should we do about it?"

As Abbey proceeded to take a sip of her coffee, the kits were alert, awaiting her answer.

Finally, she said, "I'm gonna lead a community protest."

Willie asked, "What does that mean ... protest?"

Abbey answered with an idiomatic expression. "It means make a big stink!"

Sebastian asked, "Abbey, what kind of stink is protest? Skunk spray is strong and stinky and is an excellent weapon of defense. Do you have a protest spray?"

"Ha! No, Sebastian, I'm afraid not. I don't mean that kind of stink."

"You don't?"

"No, protest isn't a liquid that can be sprayed or squirted."

Willie scratched his head. "Then what kind of defense is it?"

"Humans make a big stink differently than animals. When we're furious about something, we protest by raising our voices, not our tails. The more people who become angry about a shared concern, the stronger the expression and hence, the greater the stink."

"Hey Abbey," Sebastian suddenly said. "Ya know what? Willie's Aunt Agram visited him last night in a dream, and she told him to do something important."

"She did? Wow! Something important. Willie, is this the dream you mentioned earlier? Go ahead and tell me about it."

Willie nodded and began talking about his dream. "Okay. In my dream Aunt Agram told me I needed to help Sebastian earn his second stripe."

"Ah hah. So now you know what it is that Sebastian must do?"

"Well, my aunt said Sebastian must help you stop whatever bad is happening in Penn's Wood."

"She said that? Amazing. I could definitely use help."

Willie continued. "But she didn't tell me how I'm supposed to help Sebastian do whatever he's supposed to do to help you."

"Maybe she left a hint in the dream?"

"She did but even though I've tried, I can't figure it out."

"What was the hint? Maybe I can help."

"Really, it's more like a clue than a hint."

"Okay," said Abigail. "Tell me the clue."

"I can't, because it's hidden in a word."

"What do you mean, hidden in a word?"

Excitedly, Willie began to explain. "Aunt Agram taught my Great[15] Grandfather Mordecai how to figure things out using a special game she invented. We need to rearrange letters from one of the words in the last sentence of an important conversation."

Abigail was becoming increasingly interested. "Have you done that yet?"

"Yes, we tried, but so far none of the words worked."

Abigail said, "Tell me what sentence you chose."

"The last thing you said before you went upstairs last night sounded important to us," said Willie.

"Okay, what'd I say?"

Sebastian said, "We heard you say something like 'sink into soft pillows'."

"That's right. I was so tired all I wanted to do was take a bath and go to sleep."

Willie picked up where Sebastian left off. "So, after I tried all the words, only 'sink' seemed to have possibilities, but I still haven't solved the problem."

Abbey got excited. "Well, you're right, Willie, the answer is definitely in the word 'sink.' And I think I know what the clue is!"

Excitedly, both kits exclaimed, "You do?"

Willie was jumping up and down while Sebastian's whiskers were quivering and his heart was thumping.

Sebastian shouted, "Abbey, tell us now!"

Willie followed with, "Yeah, hurry up, tell us. Tell us the answer!"

"It's simple. Just add the letter T after the letter S in the word 'sink,' and you have stink!"

Sebastian asked, "But why the letter T?"

"It's complicated, but it has to do with the shape of the letter. I'll explain another time. What's important is that Sebastian needs to protest what's happening in Penn's Wood, just like I'm doing. Sebastian, this is just astonishing. It's the very favor I wanted to ask you last night before I went to bed. Remember?"

Sebastian, still not quite understanding said, "Yeah, so the favor is ...?"

Abbey answered, "To help me save the environment in Penn's Wood by —"

"Making a big stink!" Willie completed Abigail's thought. "Get it, Sebastian? Stink!"

Sebastian's eyes were huge and unblinking as he questioned Abigail. "You mean I'm supposed to use my skunk stink to help you in your fight?"

"Yes, exactly."

"But Abbey, I don't know how to do that yet. And I'm not sure I'm allowed to help other animal types defend themselves. Even if I am, how can one skunk defend against such a huge enemy? My arsenal of musk bullets is very limited."

Willie jumped in and asked, "And how am I supposed to help? That still hasn't been answered."

Abbey thought for a minute. "Willie, at least we've answered some of the questions. All we need to do is figure out the rest. Perhaps tonight your Aunt Agram will visit again. Maybe she'll tell you more."

Willie clasped his paws together. "Oh Abbey, I hope so."

Abbey finished her coffee, then went back upstairs with Willie in tow, while Sebastian headed to DJ's room to attempt a connection despite his failure the day before. After a quick shower, Abigail put on her bathrobe and seated herself in front of the dressing table. She wrinkled her brow and peered into the mirror. Willie was seated in his usual spot, just outside the bathroom door, listening to Abigail as she muttered to herself.

"Oh, this is not looking good. There it is, a new wrinkle across my forehead, another worry line for sure. What more can I do to fight off that land man who knocked on my door last week? He already had a lease in hand with a sizable offer, one he thinks I can't refuse.

"Well, we'll just see about that. I'll fight it all the way! I won't let them come. They'll bring those huge trucks and build their fire-breathing drill rigs with vampire-like equipment right in my back yard. The life blood of the Earth will be sucked out, and my land destroyed just like everyone else's.

"And if that isn't bad enough, what about the chemicals they pour down the rigs along with millions of gallons of our precious and dwindling water? Everyone knows the chemicals are poisonous, ruining our wells and making us all sick...including the animals. And what with the drought happening across the country, how dare they use up so much water.

"Oh, and lest I forget, where are they putting the vomit that comes back up out of the Earth after they drill? In some open wastewater pit, that's where. People say it stinks. It's causing air pollution and ruining crops. So what do they do next? They pour the gunk back in the ground which, of course, is causing all these new earthquakes. The problems and dangers just keep multiplying. I can't let them do it."

When Abigail came out of the bathroom she almost tripped over Willie. He had ventured closer to the door upon hearing her upset mutterings. Willie couldn't help but become increasingly agitated as he listened, and when she opened the door, Abigail found him huddled in a ball and shivering.

In a quivering voice Willie said, "Oh m-my stars, Abbey. I heard you talking about something b-bad that might h-happen to the land behind your house. That's where our burrow is, too."

"Yes Willie, you heard right. The food needed for things to run—like I told you and Sebastian about— is underneath Penn's Wood, and that includes the Newton homestead. They want to build drill rigs right behind my home."

Willie gasped and looked as if he would faint.

Abigail cried, "Willie, Willie," and rushed into the bathroom to get a small cup of water from the sink. After taking a few laps, Willie felt somewhat better, but the shock of Abigail's unexpected news persisted.

"Abbey, when is this supposed to happen, the trucks, the drill rigs, the digging?"

"I'm not sure. It's been happening in the forests and farmlands. I guess that wasn't enough. Now they're coming to the suburbs near homes and schools."

Willie didn't know what to say. The painful memory of losing his home and being separated from his parents came flooding in without warning, engulfing him in great sadness.

"Willie you look so depressed, and it's my fault. I didn't want to say anything about what might happen here until I had more information. But it's been on my mind and I'm sorry. I forgot you were right outside the door."

"Oh Abbey, when I left the Deep Creek, I thought all of this was behind me."

"All of what?"

"The metal monsters with long necks and flashing eyes that gobbled up the land and the den where I was born. We had to move, but my parents couldn't find a place large enough for all of us, so they sent me to live with Aunt Sylvia, Uncle Sol, and Sebastian. When we said goodbye, Mom and Dad promised to visit, but they never did."

"Willie, I had no idea."

"So now the monsters are coming to gobble up my home again?"

Abigail answered, "Yes, unless we do something. That's why I'm going to a meeting in Big City. They've made a big stink in an interesting way, and I want to find out more. It's a big deal."

Abigail headed downstairs with Willie following, stopping briefly in DJ's room where Sebastian and DJ lay napping. After stroking Sebastian once and giving DJ a kiss, she continued downstairs and into the kitchen where she said goodbye to Willie, Oliver, and the Davey-sitter.

Willie tried to ask more questions, but was cut short by Abigail. "Sorry. Gotta get going. See you all later."

Willie listened to the clicking of Abigail's heels as she went down the basement steps. Then he heard the door into the garage close, the car door, the grind of the garage door motor, and the rumble of the car. Abigail was gone, and Willie was left to ponder what she had told him. He needed to talk to Sebastian. Immediately.

Sebastian was still snuggled against DJ when Willie came into the room. "Get up, Sebastian. We need to talk."

Sebastian stirred and then blinked. "What is it, Willie?"

"Come on. Hurry. We need to figure out how I can help you help Abbey make a big stink."

"Okay, but what's the rush?"

"Here's the rush: Abbey just told me that the land where we all live will soon be under attack."

"Under attack? By who?"

"Drillers are coming to clear the land behind her home. And then they'll start digging."

"Oh for the love of the stars! But Willie, first we need to free the skunks and get back to Enlightenment School before we can help Abbey."

Willie had a sudden brainstorm. "That might be part of it," he declared.

"Part of what?"

"Maybe that's how I'm supposed to help you, by freeing the skunks."

"You could be right. Like I said, I only have so many musk bullets. Same with all the skunks. We need time to reload. Abbey said protest is stronger when many join to make a big stink. Maybe if more skunks join us—"

"Sebastian, you're brilliant! We're figuring it out together."

***

That night Aunt Agram visited Willie again. Floating through the window and into the room, she looked almost the same as she had the previous night. However, this time she was a miniature of her former ghost self. Sitting on Willie's shoulder, she spoke directly into his ear in a whispery voice.

"Willie, Abbey said Big City did a big deal. I'm here to tell you the secret word. It's deal."

The word vibrated in Willie's sleeping unconscious all night until morning when he was awakened by his own voice saying, "Deal, deal, deal."

Sebastian was also awakened by Willie's word repetitions. "Willie, what do you mean, deal?"

"Aunt Agram visited me again in my dreams. She whispered the word 'deal' and said it was the secret word."

"Okay, another clue! You better start rearranging the letters. Hurry up."

As quickly as he could, Willie joined Sebastian, who was already halfway down the steps on his way to the kitchen and Oliver's bowl. With no leftovers in which to scratch the letters, Sebastian didn't know what to do, until he noticed the muddy footprints by the back door.

"Over here, Willie. You can scratch the letters in the mud."

Hurriedly, Willie began rearranging. First he tried E-A-L-D. "Not a word."

Next he tried A-D-L-E. "Nope. What else is left?"

"Willie, I think I know. Try L-E-A-D. That might be a real word."

Willie scratched away. They both watched as the word emerged in the mud.

"That's it, Sebastian. Lead! As in, you must lead. Lead the skunks to make a really big stink."

"Me, a leader? But how?"

Willie thought for a moment and then, in a spontaneous flash of clarity, the plan came into his mind. He spoke decisively.

"The way I envision it, Sebastian, you're the leader of an army. An army of skunks. Let's call it ... Skunk Ground Forces."

"I'm not so sure, Willie," Sebastian said, shaking his head. "I've never led anything before. You're the one who's always in the lead."

"That's true, Sebastian, but now it's your turn. This is the way you'll finish earning your second stripe. It'll help Abbey and it'll save our homes. Not only that, but if you lead enough skunk forces, maybe you can save the Earth beyond Penn's Wood, maybe even all over the land."

"I'm not sure I could do that," Sebastian worried.

"Well I think you could. Might even be your destiny. After all, your Great[15] Grandfather Norton was Captain of the Skunk Salvation Seekers and you—you could be Commander of all Skunk Ground Forces, saving the environment from disaster everywhere."

"Willie! How am I gonna do that?"

"I'm not sure. Maybe when we get back to Enlightenment School, the coaches can help you with that part."

Sebastian paused and then said, "Don't forget what our kit coaches said. We aren't allowed to fight the battles of other animal types. So what if Sir doesn't think it's a good idea for me to help Abbey in her fight?"

Willie answered, "Think about it, Sebastian. This battle is not just Abbey's. It's our home in danger, too. And how about all the other animals' homes? Abbey can make a human stink while we make an animal stink. Now listen, at sundown this evening I'll start releasing the skunks from their traps. Abbey's going to buy berries and other stuff for you to feed them, so the sooner we get going, the faster we'll meet up with our coaches and figure out what to do and how to do it."

"Okay, Willie. You seem to be sure of this plan, so you can be the one to tell Abbey. In the meantime, it's Beauregard who's supposed to lead us back after we round up all the skunks. How long do you suppose it'll take? And when do you think Beauregard will return?"

"The way I figure, it should take us about three moonrises to round up all the skunks. Then another moon for them to rest up. Beauregard should be back by then."

When Abbey got back from her meeting, she was tired but excited. Big City had mustered enough support from hundreds of protesters to ban the new drilling process. She told Sebastian and Willie how Big City had written a new ordinance based on citizens' rights to clean air and clean water. However, she knew that what Big City had done was controversial and wouldn't be possible in her borough unless she got others to make a big stink along with her.

In turn, Willie told Abigail about their plan. She was thrilled to know her animal friends would help drive off the drillers, but Sebastian was still uneasy.

~ 17 ~

The Traps Are Tripped

At dusk Sebastian and Willie left Abigail's home to return to their burrow. Carrying a basket of food, Abbey followed along and dropped the food from her basket, a little at a time, into the main entrance. Willie and Sebastian filled up on some of the berries and stored the rest in a corner of the great room. Bolstered by his plan to fight the enemy, Willie felt strong and determined. Sebastian, still dubious, remained apprehensive.

Before Willie left to begin releasing the skunks, the kits gave each other brotherly hugs and wishes of good luck. As Willie wiggled up and out of the burrow, Sebastian shouted a last minute request.

"Willie, please trip the trap nearest to Abbey's house first."

Willie shouted back, "Why?"

"Because the skunkette, the one I told you about, is caught in it and she ..."

"Okay, I get it, Sebastian."

Despite his limp, Willie worked through the night, releasing as many skunks as possible from traps in the neighborhood. One at a time, he escorted each skunk back to the burrow, where Sebastian was waiting with greetings and food. By dawn twenty skunks had been released and were safe in the burrow with Sebastian. After Willie returned with the last of that night's released captives, everyone was tired and ready to sleep through the day.

Freeing the skunks took longer than originally anticipated. But finally, by the fifth night, a hundred skunks had been rounded up. All were given food and water, thanks to Abigail. Those requiring first aid were taken to Abigail for special treatments. After healing they rejoined their brethren in the backyard burrow. Only one skunk, still too weak to travel, remained behind, and her name was Sabrina. It was she who had attracted Sebastian's attention and who Willie liberated first.

Back in the burrow, the skunks were edgy, awaiting Beauregard's arrival. Finally, the general made his appearance, tunneling in from one of the burrow's north-south offshoots.

"Well, mah goodness gracious. I nevah expected to see so many skunks in one burruh. And looky here, Sebastian. Your second stripe is beginning to crawl fuhther up your back. It's at least another inch longer. You must be earnin' it, all right. It's just a matter o' time before you're a full-fledged, bona fide skunk."

Sebastian was thrilled. "Are you sure, General Beauregard? Is it really longer? Is it as bushy as the rest of my fur? Is it the same shade of white? Willie, can you see it?"

Willie, who had been gathering the skunks, came over and took a careful look. "Yup, Beauregard's right. Your second stripe has grown and it's almost as bushy, but not quite as bright, as your first stripe."

Once all the skunks were ushered into the burrow's main room, Sebastian said, "Everyone, I want you to meet our leader, General Beauregard. He's the one we've been telling you about, and he'll escort us safely back to Enlightenment School."

Sebastian stepped to the side, allowing General Beauregard to speak.

"Now, jus' gather round and listen up."

The skunks clustered around the General like a doughnut around its hole. When he held up his paw in greeting, turning fully around and then back again so all could see him, a cheer rang out. Slowly, Beauregard lowered his paw and waited for the throng to settle down. Finally, when there was a hush in the room, Beauregard cleared his throat and began to speak.

"I thank you for this glorious welcome. Now usually I am a happy go lucky fella, but I gotta tell ya, that's not the case right now. Mah travels with Sir and Coach Politella were most challenging. We had many difficulties makin' our way back to that there Enlightenment School of yours. I don' wanna take up too much time explaining, 'cept to say that there's something going on underground as well as above ground that ain't too good. Fact is, it's real bad. Took us twice as long to get where we were going than it should of, and we saw some pretty scary stuff along the way."

There was a murmur among the skunks. Sebastian asked, "General, can you tell us what was scary?"

"Well, Sebastian, I was gettin' to that." There was a hush in the room. "Ya see, I was diggin' our escape tunnel—the one we'll use to get y'all back to school starting tomorruh—when outta nowhere there came this twirling tube. It jus' kept going straight down, right in front of me. And it made this here awful noise, and the ground just shook and shook. We had ta cover our ears an' hold on ta one another 'til it stopped. Gave me and the coaches bad headaches. And we had to veer around it so as ta keep on digging the tunnel."

Willie interrupted to ask, "Was that the only bad thing?"

"Unfortunately, no, son. There was more than one o' those twirling tubes. And we encountered other tubes that didn't twirl, but ran horizontal like, along the underground. Had to keep going round them, too. The worst of it was that some o' those horizontal ones had these real fine cracks with smelly stuff seeping out. Made us cough and choke. Made our eyes sting and water. Made our whiskers burn and curl. And we done up-chucked from time to time. Ever' so often I had to tunnel us back outta the underground so's we could git us something to eat and sniff us a whiff of fresh air... well, sorta fresh air."

Sebastian asked, "What happened when you came out from the down below?"

"Interesting you should ask. It was better in some ways, but still bad. Even though the air was not as pungent as it was underground, it still smelled foul. And the fuhther south we got, well the air, it just kept gettin' worse. But at least it wasn't as suffocating as in the underground."

"How about when you got to Enlightenment School? What then?" Willie asked.

"Well, since the school is in one of them extensive burruhs, it wadn't as bad as in the tunnels. But I gotta tell ya, the animals are havin' a hard time paying attention to their kit coaches. And sometimes they miss school because o' being sick with one ailment or anothuh."

Both Willie and Sebastian gave each other side glances, not knowing what to say. There was a momentary silence, finally broken by Willie.

"Beauregard, there's stuff me and Sebastian learned from Abigail and —"

"Hold on a minute, there," Beauregard said. "I'm still not done. There's more. One time when the three of us went above, we witnessed the night sky jus' light right up. It came right outta this tower. Had a red-hot flare real high and melted the snow all around. Couldn't even see the stars twinkling, just sparks from the red-hot. Then there was this boom. Boom, boom, boom. One aftuh anothuh. We scrambled back underground and didn't come back out again 'til we made it to Enlightenment. The trip back here was not as bad because I was by mahself and traveling north, away from most of the troubles. And I'd already tunneled around them twirling tubes, plus I didn't climb out unless I absolutely had to. Howevah, now I gotta turn back around and git y'all safely to school. Jus' lemmie tell ya, we gotta be real careful on the way. I developed some important ground rules. Y'all ready to hear the rules?"

Willie interrupted, saying, "Hey, Beauregard—I mean General—don't forget we have information for you, too."

"Well, then, go ahead, son. I guess it's your turn. What's on your mind?"

Willie briefed Beauregard. "Abbey knows all about how the bad things are happening in Penn's Wood. She knows about the ground shaking, the foul smell in the air, the polluted water, the noise, the flaming towers, and how people and animals are getting sick, even dying."

Beauregard asked, "Does Miss Abbey know why this is happening?"

"Yes, she said it's from getting something called gas out of the ground."

"But what is this here gas, and what's it for?" Beauregard looked puzzled.

This time it was Sebastian who answered. "It's a kind of food needed by people machines, to make them operate. There's some new way of getting more gas out of the ground. Problem is, it's real danger-ous. And besides, once it's all used up ... well, there just isn't any more."

"No more food to make things work, you say? If that's the case, maybe people should find some-thin' besides this here gas stuff. Shall we get back to mah under-the-ground rules?"

Sebastian hesitated. "Uh, General, there's more we need to tell you."

"Like what? Tell me the whole danged mess."

"It's like this. Recently the ghost of Willie's ancient aunt came to visit him in a dream, saying I could earn the rest of my second stripe if Willie would help me help Abbey fight these gas drillers. See, they're planning on drilling right behind her house and that means our burrow."

"But how ya gonna fight such critters?"

"Abbey's gonna make a big stink and Willie's aunt said I should lead all the skunks to do the same thing."

"Whadya mean, Abbey's gonna 'make a big stink'? How's she gonna do that without a tail?"

"She said people make a big stink by raising their voices. The more people, the louder their voices. Willie figured out that the more skunks we have, the bigger and more powerful our stink."

Beauregard was astounded. "But do ya know what that'll do ta the forest? Y'all have over a hundred skunks ready to fight."

The skunks made loud squeaking noises showing their support and readiness.

Beauregard continued, "That's purt near a whole army. If that much stink is made all at once ... well, y'all are talking about a potential gas war, and you know that's prohibited."

Sebastian spoke up. "Yes, that's the main reason I'm nervous about the plan."

"Sebastian, I do understand your predicament, but that stripe o' yours is growing in even as we speak. I think it's a sign you're on the right path. But y'all need ta discuss this with your kit coaches when ya get back to school. There certainly is a conflict, one that will take some figuring out."

Sebastian did need time to think. His concern about what would happen to the forest if there were a gas war between the skunks and the drillers caused him great consternation. He was overwhelmed and needed time to sort out his feelings. But there wasn't any time. They had to prepare for the journey next dusk.

After a brief silence, Beauregard said, "Before we all retire for the day, I want to go over those important ground rules, so here goes. Number one: I'll lead the way. Sebastian and Willie will follow after me, in that order. Number two: Y'all will line up behind Willie and stay close together. Number three: each skunk must hold the tail of the skunk in front and nevah—and I mean nevah—let go. Unless I say so. Number four: only Sebastian, Willie, and me can leave the underground to get food when we don't find enough grubs along the way. And that means one at a time so y'all are nevah left without a leader. And last of all, number five: y'all must listen to Sebastian when I'm not here. He will be your primary leader. In fact, I appoint him as your commander in chief—that is, aftuh we get to Enlightenment School. If Sebastian goes missing, well then, y'all are gonna have ta take your orders from Willie, who I officially appoint as second in command."

~ 18 ~

The Journey to Enlightenment

The very next dusk, the one hundred skunks forming the first regiment were led by Beauregard, Willie, and Sebastian. They departed from the main room of the burrow and began their journey along the recently forged southern route. It took several sunrises and sunsets to reach their destination, and their arduous passage was marked by mishaps and misfortune.

The skunks were not used to being confined to an underground existence at the depth of Beauregard's Tunnel, or Tunnel B as it was finally named. Tunnel B was wide enough since it had to accommodate the largest groundhog ever to grace the land, so width was not a problem. When they first entered Tunnel B, the height of the ceiling was ample. However, it began to decrease gradually as Beauregard and the band of skunks traveled farther south. This was because the sporadic spacing of the twirling tubes had created extra work for Beauregard. While excavating the tunnel, he had dug long and wide but not high, to lessen his work load. Thus, the animals felt claustrophobic, especially since they had been instructed by Beauregard to stay close together holding on to one another's tails.

Also, they were hungrier than usual. There had been a recent and unnatural thaw, given the time of year. The ground was no longer frozen, and the tunnel floor was muddy and slippery, creating a more difficult path. Earthworms, which were usually plentiful under these circumstances, seemed to be less so within the tunnel. For this reason, all three leaders needed to seek food above ground more often.

Each time one of the three ventured out of a burrow hole to enter the vast beyond, they did so at great risk. There was the risk of being caught in an animal trap, of being eaten by hungry predators, of being shot by people hunters, or of becoming disoriented and lost. And there were the many risks created by the new industry growing across the land.

On one occasion, Sebastian came back reporting sick-looking cows roaming pastures right next to a flaming tower. And he even saw a deformed calf. Willie reported seeing young people playing across a field separated from an inferno by barbed wire fences and ominous "DANGER, KEEP OUT" signs. All three saw strange rectangular lakes of gray water with peculiar chemical smells. If that wasn't enough, there were also pools of slick grease bubbling up in nearby streams, like invisible pots simmering on top of hidden underground cauldrons.

It was almost dawn on the morning before arriving at Enlightenment School when Beauregard addressed the disheveled group.

"Okay, y'all, we're purt near your school but it's almost dawn and we need some victuals and rest before going any fuhthuh. Gonna git on our way again at dusk tomorruh aftuh break-the-fast. But right now it's dinnuh time. According ta mah record keeping, it seems ta be Willie's turn to get us some grub."

"You're right, General," Willie answered, "and it's a good thing, because we're all getting hungry. So let me know when you spot the next dugout and I'll skedaddle up, as you like to put it."

Beauregard was quick to respond and jerked his head upward, pointing with his snout. "Up is right here and up is right now and up is ... Hell's Bells."

Willie looked up and was not surprised to see a burrow hole opening since Beauregard had, like a transportation conductor, announced each of the tunnel's exits along the way. Hell's Bells was the next to last exit, the last one being Enlightenment School. Beauregard called out conductor style, "This exit, Hell's Bells!"

Willie looked at Beauregard and said "Hell's Bell's? Why such a funny name? Are you kidding me? Who would want to stop here with a name like that?"

Beauregard answered, "I know, but that's what I named it, because when I went out, all hell was a-breaking loose, with all kinds of activity a-buzzing. But we gotta do what we gotta do, so Willie, be real careful!"

"Okay, don't you worry. I'll be back in no time with dinner for all."

Sebastian watched as Willie wriggled out. "Goodbye! And don't forget, no wandering off."

But Willie didn't hear Sebastian. He was too preoccupied with the mission of foraging for food. Once he saw the landscape in front of him, however, his hunger dried up. He was so unnerved by what he saw that each hair stood on end as if electrified.

* * *

It had been an early morning when Willie delivered Sabrina to Abigail. From the moment she saw the small animal curled up in Willie's protective paws, Abigail felt a kinship. But Sabrina couldn't open her eyes, lift her limp tale, or eat. Abigail wasn't sure she could nurse this small-boned skunkette back to health. Choosing not to cage the lifeless kit, Abigail tucked Sabrina into a basket lined with a small soft coverlet.

After several unsuccessful attempts to rouse the skunkette, Abigail called Dr. Murphy and was on the phone when the Davey-sitter arrived. As he walked past on his way to DJ's bedroom for morning care, he nodded a greeting to Abigail.

Abigail smiled in relief at his timely arrival and spoke into the phone. "Okay, Jack, I'll bring her in immediately...Yeah, I kind of thought you would recommend intravenous feeding. I agree she's probably dehydrated ... Oh, her name? Don't know. I'm not getting any intuitive signals, and that's a bad sign. Okay, see you soon."

Abigail laid her hand on Sabrina. She could feel the weak flutter of Sabrina's heart and the dampness of her fur. Abigail thought the little thing must have a fever. Hurriedly, she wrapped Sabrina in a small blanket, tucked her into the lined basket, then yelled to the Davey-sitter, "I'm on my way to the animal hospital."

When they arrived, Abigail whisked the basket off the car seat and took Sabrina into the clinic, where a technician was waiting for the suffering animal.

Abigail had only been in the waiting room for a short while when Dr. Murphy stuck his head out the clinic door. "Come on in, Abbey."

"Thanks, Jack." She walked through the door and into the clinic, where he directed her down to one of the pre-op rooms.

"We've already got your skunk ready to be hooked up to an intravenous drip. Not only is she dehydrated, but she's also suffering from malnutrition and running a fever."

Abbey looked at Dr. Murphy. "Do you think she'll be okay?"

"Not sure. I'll know more in a couple of hours, after I see how she tolerates the intravenous. Go on home and I'll call you when I know more."

"Hmmm, you know, Jack, I didn't have time for breakfast this morning. Think I'll go over to the Pitt Stop. I need some coffee, and maybe I'll treat myself to one of their famous pecan rolls."

"Okay, but don't come back without bringing one for me. In the meantime, while you're there, relax, read the paper, and people watch. By the time you get back I should know more about the status of your new little friend."

Abigail answered, "It's a plan."

The morning had been brisk but dry, with a cloudless blue sky, so Abigail decided to walk. Taking a deep breath of crisp fresh air, she began her walk, admiring the snow-lined rooftops as she moved toward her destination. The cafe, scented with cinnamon and coffee, was a welcome retreat. Abigail had been a regular customer before DJ became sick. It was her special place to sit and write stories for her grandson Simon. Shirley, the hostess, recognized Abigail right away and greeted her warmly.

"Abbey, what the heck! We were just talking about you the other day. Saw your picture in the local paper. So now you're a celebrity. Too good for us, huh? Where've you been, anyway?"

Abigail was embarrassed. She shrugged. "Don't be silly. I've just been real busy, but I'm here now, and it's good to see all of you. How about getting me a cup of coffee and a pecan roll, toasted please, no butter. Oh, make that two pecan rolls, one to go. Thanks."

"Okay, come on. Follow me. Your favorite spot by the window is waiting for you."

Shirley led Abigail to a corner banquette surrounded by windows with red and white gingham curtains. Red plastic geraniums in brown clay pots lined the sill. The spot was comforting, being across from a fireplace where the glowing embers flared and crackled. It created just the cozy atmosphere Abigail needed. She was flooded with fond memories.

As Abigail slid in, Shirley said, "I'll be right back with your order and a copy of a certain newspaper article I saved for you."

"Thanks, Shirley."

"Oh, no problem. Maybe we can talk about it. That is, if you want. Besides, I could use a break.

All the customers have been waited on, so we can chat. What do you say?"

"Listen Shirley, that depends on which side you're on. The subject is beyond controversial, and people are drawing lines in the sand. I'm not in the mood for a debate, much less an argument."

"Not to worry. I agree with everything they quoted you as saying at that meeting."

Abigail nodded. "Sure, then we can talk about it."

Abigail watched Shirley walk in the direction of the kitchen, relieved to have some breathing room before Shirley's return. All Abigail wanted to do was feel the warmth of the fire, watch the dancing flames, and listen to the spitting and hissing of the burning wood as it shifted during its disintegration.

Shirley returned with their food. As Abigail nibbled the pecan roll and sipped the freshly brewed coffee, Shirley read portions of the recent newspaper article titled "Local Woman Raises Concerns."

At last night's public hearing, Abigail Newton, a resident of South Penn's Wood and outspoken critic of unconventional natural gas drilling, also known as fracking, discussed one of the many complex problems faced by land owners.

According to Mrs. Newton, there are multiple issues when it comes to land leasing for drilling. "For starters, there's the question of land ownership. One would think that's obvious, but it's not," she stated. "Complications occur when one person owns surface rights but someone else owns mineral rights. It's the minerals under the surface that the drilling companies are after. Problem is, the greatest risks are at the surface, where a home is built, crops are grown, animals graze, and children play. There's little or no compensation for the surface rights owner."

When asked about the risks, Newton was quick to answer. "The land itself is destroyed. Homes and property values are damaged. Air and water are polluted. Health and wellness suffer. Fact is, the Earth itself is at risk for greater global warming, now called climate change."

Newton also spoke about the challenge of forced pooling which can occur when drilling companies can make a landowner who is unwilling to lease their land, join with neighbors who are willing to lease. "That's what's happening in my neighborhood right now," Newton said. "I don't intend to lease my land, but I'm being forced to sign on the dotted line."

In response to a question of what she intends to do about it, Newton said, "Make a big stink!'"

Shirley stopped reading, put down the paper, and began firing questions. "So Abbey, what will you do? How do you plan to make a big stink? With a sling shot and some stones? You realize you're up against a Goliath, don't you? And, by the way, how are things with your neighbors? I hear it can get really ugly."

Abigail took a deep breath. "All I can say is it's very contentious. Some neighbors won't speak to me, and others are calling and asking how they can help fight what seems to be an inevitable curse."

"Inevitable? Obviously you plan on doing something. But you haven't answered my question yet. Exactly how will you make the big stink?"

"I have help, but I can't discuss it now. Besides, you wouldn't believe it even if I told you!"

Shirley laughed. "Oh Abbey, you are one for the books. I know you've got something up your sleeve. I also know you won't tell me until you're good and ready, so there's no sense my bothering you about it any longer. By the way, how's DJ?"

Relieved in one way that Shirley changed the subject, but not happy about the topic of choice, Abigail's brusquely answered, "Not good."

Shirley could tell there was nothing more to be said and that their conversation had come to an abrupt end. "Well, break time is over, and I've got to get back to work. You take care and don't be a stranger. Say hi to DJ for me."

"Thanks for the chat and the extra newspaper. I'll be sure to tell DJ hello," Abigail said, despite knowing that her husband hadn't been able to understand a hello from a goodbye for months. She sat for awhile, allowing herself to be hypnotized by the flames lapping around the shifting logs until they burned into embers and transformed to ash. Her trance was broken when her cell phone rang.

"Hi, Abbey. It's Susie from Murphy's Animal Hospital. Dr. Murphy said you can return. Your little skunk has come around. Seems the IV did the trick, and at least now she's responsive. One of our techs even gave her some food and she kept it down."

"Thanks, I'll leave now. It'll take me about ten minutes to walk back."

Abigail put on her hat, coat, and gloves. She grabbed the newspaper and extra pecan roll and left the diner.

* * *

At the Hell's Bells exit, a stunned Willie stood erect on his hind legs, looking out at the landscape. What he saw dredged up an old and frightening memory. The sprawling terrain was crawling with machines, larger versions of those he had seen in the Deep Creek. Back then, Willie was terrified by the one-eyed monsters spewing smoke while gouging immense holes in the earth. But these machines were much larger, accompanied by massive trucks. Interspersed among the machines and trucks, Willie saw towers, all with "red-hots blowin' their tops" as Beauregard had described. Loud whooshing sounds came from each of them during bursts of angry flares.

It was as if the Earth was one big unhappy birthday cake lighting up the night sky, with more flaming candles than could ever be blown out. Willie wondered how he would ever find food in this hideous place, besieged with vehicles, towers, flames, and fumes. He began to shiver all over and had trouble breathing, either from fear or fumes, or both.

Overwhelmed by instinct and without giving thought to the dangers ahead, Willie limped forward, attempting to challenge the strange land-destroying enemies. He was driven to tear apart the machines with his claws, bite them with his teeth, and poison them with his weasel sputum. He was limping as fast as he possibly could when a deafening explosion occurred.

Willie came to an abrupt halt, whiskers twitching, fur on end, and tail stiff. In the distance he saw a fireball of immense proportions roll in the direction of several farm houses on the edge of what was once a pastoral scene, now morphed into an ugly industrial landscape. Staring, he watched as all three homes burst into flame. People ran everywhere. Sirens wailed. It was absolute chaos.

Wanting to help, Willie moved toward the turmoil. As he got closer, one of the sparks shooting from the fireball scorched his fur, singeing the tip of each hair of his white winter coat, making him look like a burnt marshmallow. Despite the possibility that his fur could catch fire, Willie forged ahead into the smoke billowing from the burning houses until he became part of the landscape's inferno.

* * *

With stomachs rumbling and mouths dry, the bedraggled underground group anxiously awaited Willie's return. They were gathered around the Hell's Bells exit hole when the ground above them shook with a loud but muffled blast. Gripped by fear, the skunks broke out into loud shrill squeaks and let go of one another's tails despite Sebastian's attempt to calm them.

Beauregard took over. "Now listen up. I say, listen up! Git hold of yurselves. This is no time ta panic, you hear? Grab those tails! Something's happened out there, and Willie's not back. Our concern needs ta be for Willie."

In response to Beauregard's words, Sebastian was so shocked that his fur bristled as if he had touched a live wire. "Beauregard, I'm going out. I need to find Willie. He may be lost or even hurt."

"Okay, Sebastian. Go ahead. After all, you are the leader of the skunks. Willie's like a brother and I understand. Go on now and see if you can determine his whereabouts. But Sebastian, I want ya ta be careful out there. Something mighty ugly seems to be happening."

Sebastian scurried up and out of the exit hole and was dumbfounded by what he saw, just as Willie had been. Unlike Willie, Sebastian's instinct had nowhere to go. Instead, he was overcome by grief, unable to imagine Willie surviving such an inferno. He stood there and began to weep, silently at first and then with a moan, followed by a scream. When Beauregard heard Sebastian's screaming, he climbed out to check. He found Sebastian standing motionless, with tears streaming from his eyes matting the fur on his face, and in a state of shock.

Beauregard tapped Sebastian gently, but Sebastian did not move. "Come on along now, Sebastian. I see the same thing you're looking at, but what I don't see is Willie. We can't leave all the skunks and go looking for him. And I don't think he'll be finding us. I know this is very hard on you, but it should help you to resolve what's gotta be done. Earn that second stripe like Willie would want ya ta do."

Beauregard embraced Sebastian and led him back down the exit hole. The anxious skunks gathered around, wanting to know what had happened.

After a brief hush, Beauregard said, "Willie's gone and I don't think he'll be coming back."

~ 19 ~

Sabrina

By the time Abigail left the cafe to return to the animal hospital, the sky had turned a shadowy gray. It had grown colder and was beginning to snow. Wind whipped at Abigail's package, as if trying to snatch it from her hands, and walking was difficult.

Abigail spoke into the wind, which seemed to grab at her words, blowing them elsewhere. "Trying to steal my pecan roll are you?"

She held the bag close to her body, protecting its contents. With a sudden surge of anger against the wind, she turned around and began walking backwards in defiance. When Abigail finally got to the animal hospital, she shoved the door open, entered, kicked it closed, and triumphantly held the bag up in the air as if displaying a trophy.

Susie asked, "What's the prize?"

Abigail looked at the dangling wet bag. "It's one of the Pitt Stop's most coveted pastries. I brought it for Dr. Murphy."

"Great. I'll grab some coffee and meet you in his office. Go on back; he's waiting for you."

By the time Abigail had removed her coat and hung it up, Susie had delivered the coffee to Dr. Murphy's office. Abigail entered, pecan roll in hand, and greeted him.

"Brought you your treat!"

"Thanks, Abbey. It's just what I need after this long day. So many sick animals and emergencies because of the weather. Sit down and have a cup of coffee with me and we can chat."

Abigail settled herself in a brown leather chair facing Dr. Murphy's large desk. "So Jack, tell me about the skunkette."

"She began to come around after we hydrated her. Initially her animal noises were weak, but they seemed to get stronger after we gave her some food. I think she's trying to tell us something. Unfortunately, I don't have your gift. How about I have the technician bring her here so you two can have a chat before leaving? I would very much like to know what she's been trying to say. Also, see if you can find out her name."

"Sure, I'll be happy to. Then I can take her home, yes?"

"I don't see why not. You know how to take care of her and she'll be better off in your home than here at the clinic."

The technician, holding a small cage with a sleeping Sabrina, knocked on the office door.

"Come on in. You can set the cage right here on my desk."

The technician did just that, and then left, closing the door.

"Well let's see, Abigail. The animal certainly looks better than when you brought her in."

"Yes, I can't believe the difference. Obviously she's tired, but very much alive. Her breathing is steady and even her fur looks somewhat revived. Shall I wake her up?"

"Go ahead."

Abigail opened the cage door, reached her hand inside, and stroked Sabrina, who blinked and then opened her eyes.

"There, there, sweet one. You've been through so much, but now you're safe and will be well cared for."

Sabrina made a few squeaks.

"Ah, yes, I know it's been very scary."

Sabrina squeaked again, only longer and in varied pitches.

"Can you say that again? I'm not sure I understood. Sounds like you said something about another skunk."

Sabrina squeaked a little louder.

"Oh, you want to know about the skunk you saw while you were trapped? And the weasel that helped you escape? Well, they're actually cousins. The skunk's name is Sebastian and the weasel's name is Willie, and both left several days ago for Enlightenment School."

Sabrina curled into a ball, tucking her head under her tail. She made some muffled animal noises that sounded mournful.

Abigail said, "Don't worry. They'll be back by the time you're well again. You haven't missed your chance to thank them...What's that?"

Sabrina changed her position, uncurling from under her tail. She stretched out, lifted her head, and looked right into Abigail's eyes before squeaking again.

Abigail smiled and with a twinkle in her eye said, "Oh, so you think you and Sebastian made a connection? How very interesting. If that's the case, I'd better get you home and spruce you up."

Dr. Murphy, always astounded by the conversations he witnessed between Abigail and various animals in his clinic, shook his head in near disbelief and then said, "Abbey, it's getting late. How about you and—what is her name?

Sabrina made three small squeaks in a row.

"Oh Jack, she just told us her name. It's Sabrina."

"Wow ... Sabrina. Well how about you and Sabrina get going? You can let me know how she's doing. I'll give you some samples of an antibiotic and some vitamins. That should do it for now. You know what to do. Push the fluids and mini meals as tolerated. I'll have the technician wrap her in a thermal blanket before you leave. You can keep the cage.

"Thanks, Jack."

Abigail took Sabrina into her home, and started conditioning her to stay with DJ during the night. She hoped Sabrina's presence would replace the sense of comfort he lost when Sebastian left.

Sabrina began to put on weight. Her fur, once matted and dull, was thick and shiny. Her eyes, which had been red and blurred, were now bright and alert. And her fearful demeanor had been replaced by a playful manner.

Every morning Abigail brushed Sabrina's fur until it shone, chatting all the while as best friends might do. They plotted and planned the expected reunion with Sebastian, and each day that went by without his or Willie's return provided yet one more opportunity for a practice session.

"Sabrina, you look beautiful. Your fur is just exquisite, and it feels like satin."

Sabrina peered into Abigail's mirror, turning this way and that as she admired herself. Her fur had just been shampooed and brushed until it radiated. And her white stripes, now nearly neon, glowed against the ebony of her head and back.

Instructing Sabrina, Abigail said, "Here, turn around, look at your tail."

Sabrina twisted her body and head around until she was able to see her tail, which was quite bushy and unusually long.

"Okay now, lift that tail of yours as high as you can. Don't forget to swish it back and forth like I told you yesterday."

Sabrina did as Abigail instructed.

"Slower now, your swishing must be slow and inviting. Oh, and while you're at it, tilt your head a little to the side and cast your eyes downward. That'll make you look shy. Sebastian's sure to find you irresistible."

"Do you really think so?" Sabrina asked hopefully.

"Absolutely. Your inner and outer beauty will beguile him. Besides, don't forget what I told you

last week. Your union with Sebastian was prede-
termined."

Abigail recalled the conversation ...

"I'm curious Sabrina, how you came by such
a lovely name? Did you know it means Legendary Princess?"

"Yes. I was named after my Great[15] Grandmother
Celeste and she was just that, a Legendary Princes."

"Celeste? The name sounds familiar. Do you
know more?"

"Yes. She was mated to Captain Norton Bulymur,
the first to discover the skunk's protective stink and
the developer of its use. It was he who brought all
the skunks from the ancient land of Westphalia to
start a new life. None of us skunks would be here
if it hadn't been for the Captain and my Great[15]
Grandmother Celeste."

Suddenly Abigail realized why the name Celeste
sounded familiar. "Oh my goodness! Do you have
any idea what this means?"

"Yes, it means that I'm special and need to live
up to my name."

"That's true, but there's more. Way more."

"What do you mean? Like what, more?"

"Okay, here goes. Now don't be shocked, but
Sebastian is a direct descendant of the same Cap-
tain Norton Bulymur that was mated to your Great[15]
Grandmother Celeste in the ancient times. You see,
my dear, Captain Norton Bulymur is Sebastian's
Great[15] Grandfather. So you both have the same
Great[15] Grandparents."

Sabrina's jaw dropped. After giving Sabrina a
moment to reflect on this revelation, Abigail con-

tinued. "Sabrina, there have been, and will continue to be, events throughout the ages that are unexplainable. And I guess this is one of them. You and Sebastian are meant for one another. This was decided eons ago."

~ 20 ~

Enlightenment

There was anguish among the skunks following the tragedy at Hell's Bells. After the explosion and Willie's disappearance, all were numb, but it didn't take long for anger to replace shock. Having experienced a personal wrong, the skunks felt the need for retribution. This fortified their allegiance to one another and to their leader, Sebastian.

Three facts had been firmly established. First, an enemy was present. Second, it was destroying the land and its inhabitants. And third, they had lost Willie and needed to fight. What the skunks didn't know was how to fight against such a powerful foe. For Sebastian, Willie's loss strengthened his resolve to help Abigail in her struggle. Until then, he hadn't fully concluded that the enemy of the people and the enemy of the animals were one and the same.

By the time Sebastian and the rest of the skunks reached Enlightenment School, they were already enlightened. Only one lesson was left to learn, and that was how to fight this deadly enemy.

When the skunks reached the final exit, Beauregard announced, "Here, here, here! We're finally here. That means we have arrived at the last exit which just happens ta be Enlightenment. So, all out for Enlightenment."

Linked paw to tail, with Sebastian in the lead and Beauregard taking up the rear, they scrambled up and out of the underground. It was dawn, but the sky was overcast, and a pungent odor permeated the air. The animals could see a trail of smoke in the distance, coming from the still burning explosion at Hell's Bells. All stood waiting for Beauregard to emerge and guide them to the school.

"Before I escort ya ta school this evening, we need to git us some food and rest. Aftuh all, I cannot send y'all to Enlightenment School looking the way ya do. Gotta clean up and be presentable. Y'all wanna make a good impression on the kit coaches and the rest of the classes, don't ya? So the first thing we need ta do is get us some victuals. Then we can meet at the pond across the way and wash up. After that, it's shuteye!"

The skunks dispersed and foraged for food, which they each consumed separately before meeting at the pond. Together they bathed in a pool of water which, although not potable, was suitable for bathing. They managed to wash away most of the underground's mud and grime from their fur, and then settled down for a good day's sleep.

At dusk Beauregard roused everyone and led them to the entrance of Enlightenment School. In a loud voice he announced, "It's time for me ta depart. Gotta move on because there's a heap o' work that's gotta get done. Howevah, nevah fear. I shall return."

Sebastian was surprised by what he thought was a hasty decision by Beauregard. "Aren't you going to lead us into Enlightenment? After all, you are the general."

"I will always be General Beauregard Lee of the Ground Hog Southern Tier. But Sebastian, you are now the leader of any and all skunk troops. Don't go forgetting your title: Commander in Chief of the Skunk Ground Forces. And yessiree, this here's your first skunk troop! In fact, I will so name it thus."

Beauregard cleared his throat. "Aftuh much deliberation I dub y'all the First Troop of the Skunk Ground Forces under the leadership of our distinguished Commander in Chief, Sebastian."

Sebastian pushed himself up on his hind feet so that he was standing upright. He took a deep breath, expanding his chest to assume a more authoritative air, and saluted General Beauregard, who saluted back.

Turning smartly to face the skunks, Sebastian said, "Atten...tion! First Skunk Troop! On the count of four, I'll lead you into Enlightenment. Ready! One. Two. Three. Four."

And the skunks, following Sebastian, marched down the burrow opening and into the school.

Beauregard watched as each disappeared down the entrance hole. Before making his own departure, he bent down and yelled into the hole.

"This here is General Beauregard Lee telling y'all to be careful and wishing y'all good luck." Then he added, "Until we meet again."

Sebastian and the rest of the skunks landed in the school's reception hall, known as the Oval. It was a large space surrounded by doors leading to a variety of classrooms, and although it was usually occupied by many animals moving about, it was empty when the skunks arrived. Again Sebastian cleared his throat, adjusted his vocal timbre, and said, "Atten...tion!"

Just then Sir and Coach Politella made their entrance from opposite ends of the Oval.

Sir greeted them first. "Sebastian! It's you! Finally, you're here. I presume all these skunks are the ones Willie freed from those terrible traps."

"Yes. Allow me to introduce you to the First Skunk Troop of the official Skunk Ground Forces."

"I, along with Coach Politella, welcome you and your First Skunk Troop to Enlightenment School. Know that the distinction of being first will always belong to you. All other ground forces will follow your example."

Sebastian asked, "Sir, what do you mean by all others?"

"We're going to need many more troops to accomplish our mission and they, in turn, will be numbered in ascending order."

"Where will they be?"

"All over the land. But don't get too far ahead of yourself. You'll learn about the plan in time —"

"We can explain it later," Coach Politella interrupted. "But Sir just mentioned Willie, and I want to know the whereabouts of my student, that mischievous weasel."

Sebastian's face fell. When his eyes turned red and teary, Sir and Coach Politella braced for what they knew would be bad news.

"Sebastian, what happened? What happened to Willie? Where is he?" Coach Politella asked.

His questions were reiterated by Sir. "What on Earth happened? We need to know!"

"He ... he ..." Sebastian began. Then his throat closed.

Sir said, "There, there, Sebastian. Take a deep breath and let it out slowly. I'll get some water."

Sir left and returned quickly with a bowl of water. After a few laps, Sebastian caught his breath and started speaking.

"There was this ex-explosion. We heard a bl-blast when we were in the underground below the Hell's Bell's exit. It was Willie's turn to get food. He was already up there when we heard a very loud boom. We waited for Willie, but... he never returned."

Sebastian gasped for air, took a few more laps of water, and then continued. "When I crawled out to look for him, I saw flames and heavy smoke not far off. I figured Willie must have gotten caught up in the catastrophe."

Sir asked, "What did Beauregard think?"

Sebastian stifled a sob. "He said, 'Willie's gone, and I don't think he'll be coming back.'"

Coach Politella spoke next. "Sebastian, do you think Willie's dead?"

"I think yes...but maybe he's just hurt real bad. Maybe he can't move or find his way back. Willie has an awful sense of direction."

Sir said, "Sebastian, I know your love for Willie is strong, and you must let that keep hope alive. But even if Willie never returns to the physical world, you'll always carry him in your heart and mind. He will always be with you in spirit, especially when you need him most. And you may be needing him sooner than you think."

"Sir, what do you mean?"

"We all know that awful things are happening around us," Sir answered. "What we kit coaches have learned is this. To put it bluntly, the land and what's underneath it is being used up. You might even say it's being killed. We have news that the same thing that's happening in Penn's Wood is happening everywhere. I'm talking destruction and pollution, forest by forest, field by field, stream by stream, river by river, and mountain by mountain, including the air above and the ground below. The land is sick, really sick. It has something like Old Hamsters Disease."

"Old Hamsters Disease? That's what DJ has," Sebastian said.

Sir continued. "Don't forget what Abbey told you, that DJ's illness started long ago. Remember, she said first the destruction of his brain was slow, and no one noticed. But with time, the disease advanced faster and faster. Now it's too late for DJ."

"Yes, he's very sick. And he looked weak and pale the last time I saw him. But, Sir, how do you know the land is being destroyed everywhere?" Sebastian asked.

"We were informed by the esteemed General Beauregard Lee himself, who has been in touch with groundhogs both near and far. You see, he is part of an important underground movement. Not only are the groundhogs outstanding civil engineers, able to communicate with one another through their network of tunnels, but they can predict weather patterns as well. According to Beauregard and his many friends, there's been an increase in the temperature, both above and below the ground, setting off unprecedented wild weather systems. That's bad news! And there's more bad news. The groundhogs have reported seeing a rapid increase in those bothersome twirling tubes."

"Twirling tubes?" Sebastian asked. "I recall Beauregard mentioning them, but I never saw one."

"That's right. You didn't see them during your underground travels because Beauregard had already completed the rerouting. During the building of Tunnel B, whenever we came upon a twirling tube, he would dig around the interference. That way you weren't hampered by them."

"Yes that's what Beauregard told us. But, where do these tubes come from?"

Coach Politella had the answer. "Sir and I snooped around to find out their origin. They come down from up above, starting in the center of each of those flaming towers you saw."

"Why do they twirl?" Sebastian wanted to know.

This time Sir responded. "Because they're drills, and twirling is what they do."

"Abbey talked about drills and drilling but I still don't know much about them or why they twirl."

Sir continued. "A drill is a special kind of digging tool. It digs a bore hole deep into the Earth. Kind of like miner bees dig, only way deeper."

One question begat another and another until Sebastian understood the whole problem and its dangerous ramifications.

Finally Sir said, "Sebastian, if what is happening to the land isn't stopped immediately, Earth will suffer the same outcome as DJ."

"You mean the land will die?"

"In some places, the land is already dead. That means plants and animals, too. All the animals are at great risk. If the Earth goes, so go its inhabitants."

Sebastian was not surprised. "I know. Abbey told me the same thing and she's rounding up her neighbors to make her own big stink. It's called pro-testing."

"Then you already know that making a big stink is exactly what the skunks need to do, too. You'll learn more about the plan in your final lesson, which be-gins tomorrow evening. Right now it's best that you and the First Skunk Troop take the rest of the night off. You can start your lessons at dusk tomorrow."

"Thank you, Sir. Given what we've been through, this is indeed a welcome decision. But can I ask you something else?"

"Sure, Sebastian, go ahead."

"What do you mean by final lesson?"

Sir answered, "It's Lesson Five from *Die Skunk die Kunst der Verteidigun.*"

"What's die Kunst ... uh, what you just said?"

"Translated, it means **The Skunk's Art of De-fense**. It was written by your Great[15] Grandfather,

Captain Norton Bulymur. The famous treatise took several round moons to finish. Legend has it that Captain Norton didn't eat, drink, or sleep until the instruction manual was finished. It contains five main chapters, each comprising a lesson that needs to be learned before entering into any kind of confrontation. And all the lessons include the Three R's of Respect, Responsibility, and Resolution."

~ 21 ~

The Skunk's Art
of Defense

The first rays of sunlight had splintered the sky into morning hues of rosy pink by the time the exhausted First Skunk Troop called it a night. Only a few skunks continued reviewing what their foggy future as soldiers might hold, while the rest of the troops drifted off to sleep.

Sebastian, still grieving over Willie, was despondent and also nervous about the title of Commander in Chief, which he felt had been thrust upon him. Not able to relax, he climbed out of the school's large underground space and began roaming about aimlessly. First he fidgeted with twigs, nosed pebbles, and then nibbled plants, all the while wondering what he and the First Skunk Troop would learn during the final lesson.

Mumbling, he reasoned to himself, "How can this be the final chapter? I only recall having had one, the one on Ethics. So if Ethics was Lesson One, what were Two, Three, and Four? When did I learn these? And what will be revealed in Five?"

Finally with unanswered questions still spinning in his head, Sebastian returned to the school's entrance, crawling back into the burrow where he found the First Skunk Troop curled up and asleep. With nothing left to do, Sebastian circled a few times before settling down and positioning his nose beneath his tail. Within minutes he joined the slumbering party.

At dusk, Sebastian and the First Skunk Troop were led into a large dining hall for a simple break-the-fast. After the meal, Coach Politella instructed the First Skunk Troop to follow him into one of the larger classrooms while Sir beckoned Sebastian to join him in his private study, located down one of the longer of the burrow's branches.

"Sebastian, I hope you're refreshed and ready for this last chapter."

"Yes, Sir. I just hope I can achieve the goal you, Beauregard, and especially Willie, established for me. That is, to develop into a real Commander, not just one in name."

"You will, Sebastian. Don't forget, you were our prize pupil."

"But Sir, I'm puzzled. I recall the first lesson, the one about ethics. But I don't remember any others. What happened to Chapters Two, Three, and Four?"

"You learned them indirectly, through experience. You might say they were life chapters rather than school chapters."

"Could you tell me the when and the what about these chapters?"

"Okay, Sebastian. Let's start by looking at the five chapter headings in *The Skunk's Art of Defense.*

Chapter One, as you said, is about ethics, Making Ethical Decisions. Chapter Two is Identifying the Enemy. Chapter Three, Knowing When to Spy. And Chapter Four is Fight or Flight. That leaves us Chapter Five, Strategic Planning. It's Strategic Planning that we are about to discuss."

Lost in thought, Sebastian wrinkled his thick bushy brow, puckered his mouth in a pensive pout, and stiffened his tail before responding. "Well, obviously there is an enemy. Yes, that's been established. However, I don't recall spying, which you say is Chapter Three's lesson."

"Think about the times you overheard Abigail reading the paper or when you overheard that conversation among the farmers."

Sebastian appeared surprised. "We were just listening. Is listening the same as spying?"

"Good question, Sebastian. Here you must apply ethics. You did not reveal your presence, and you continued to listen, probably because you felt the information was important. In that case, I would call it spying."

Sebastian nodded. "I see what you mean, Sir."

"So—and this is important, Sebastian—Willie understood that what was heard by your inadvertent spying confirmed a shared enemy between you and Abigail. Further, he knew that to win, you and Abigail needed to join forces in fighting the common enemy."

With the mention of Willie, Sebastian's throat got tight and his voice cracked. "Sir, Willie is...was... really the w-wise one. He kept telling me that we didn't need to go to school to become enlightened, that experience was our t-teacher."

Sir looked Sebastian square in the face before resuming the conversation. "Willie was partly correct. Because of his weasel ways, you learned what's in Chapters Two, Three, and Four. But Chapters One and Five can only be learned in school. So, are you ready for Strategic Planning?"

"Yes, Sir!"

Sir began the lesson. "First of all, strategic plans must be individualized. Each defensive situation varies according to circumstances. The circumstances in this case involve the destruction of our land by cunning managers in the drilling industry."

"Okay, I'm listening. What should I do and how should I direct the First Skunk Troop?"

Sir continued. "You will lead the First Skunk Troop through Tunnel B back to your burrow on the Newton property. Once you're settled, you must confer with Abigail and let her in on the plan since she plays a critical role."

"What more does Abbey need to do? She's already organizing her neighbors and fighting her borough council."

"Sebastian, Abigail must be responsible for making sure you and the other skunks have enough food and water while you remain underground. It would be risky to emerge from your burrow until you're ready to challenge the drillers. You might get caught in one of the traps, captured, or even killed."

"But we can't stay underground forever."

"It won't be forever. I promise. You'll emerge when the fleet of trucks and machines arrive to start clearing the land."

Sebastian asked, "But how will we know when that happens?"

"We're made with a special inner ear even though our outer ears are small. When the machines arrive, you'll hear their loud rumble and feel the vibrations of the ground trembling long before any humans hear it. That's your signal to surface. Unfortunately, there isn't any advanced warning. The drillers can start their work almost anytime, day or night."

"So we must always be ready, right?"

"Right!"

Sebastian had more questions. "Okay. So now I know when to crawl out. But do I go first, followed by the First Troop or the other way around?"

Sir paused for a moment before answering. "Ah, another good question. That part of the Strategic Plan, my friend, is being left up to General Beauregard Lee and his underground fleet of engineers. He will advise you accordingly."

"You mean Beauregard is coming back that soon?"

"Yes, Beauregard will greet you and the First Skunk Troop upon your return to the Newton property."

"Oh, that's fantastic news! I already miss him, even though he just left. And so do the rest of the skunks. Come to think of it, he did say something about seeing us again. So what comes next?"

"When the enemy comes onto the land, you and the First Skunk Troop will exit the burrow from wherever General Beauregard decides is the most advantageous location. Obviously, you are in the lead and will have already instructed First Troop to line up side by side facing the enemy once the entire troop is out of the burrow. When the machines are within shooting distance, command your troop to negotiate first by warning the enemy. Always try to negotiate first."

"Okay, Sir, but how do we warn them? How do we negotiate?"

"There are several warning signals. Begin by hissing in unison. If that's not enough, start stomping your front paws. These threat behaviors put the enemy on notice, and believe me, they'll know what comes next if they don't retreat."

"Sir, how hard, how loud, and for how long should we stomp?"

"Don't worry about that. Every skunk knows, by instinct, how to start softly and then crescendo into a noisy percussion until the enemy recognizes this as the almost final warning sign."

Sebastian looked puzzled. "What if these threats aren't enough to drive off the machines and trucks? You said that it's the almost final warning signal. Is there something else?"

"Yes, Sebastian, there's one last warning. Command your forces to turn around, and lift their tails in unison, but —"

"But, Sir, if we all shoot our musk bullets at the same time, it'll cause pollution in the forest as bad or worse than what the gas drilling might cause. It would be chemical warfare, the very thing my Great[15] Grandfather wanted to avoid."

"True, Sebastian, but you interrupted me. I was about to say that if lifting tales in unison still doesn't work, only one skunk shoots. That would be the commander, and that's you, Sebastian. Your first musk shot becomes the obvious final warning. When the enemy smells a single spray and realizes what another one hundred skunks could potentially do, they will retreat. It's a given."

"But what if they don't?"

"We have planned for that possibility. If they don't withdraw, instruct the skunk next to you to shoot and so it will go, one skunk at a time on down the line until the enemy is gone. And go they will!"

Sebastian still looked uncertain. "What if we use up all our bullets? What then?"

Sir answered, "That'll never happen. One very important thing to remember: it takes about ten days for your musk bullets to recharge. With one hundred skunks comprising First Troop, you have enough to hold the enemy off indefinitely. But that won't be necessary. Beauregard figures the workmen cannot withstand more than five stink bullets at a time."

"So we win the Battle of Newton Hill and help Abigail, but what happens after that? In other places?"

"Okay, Sebastian, now for the rest of the plan. This is where General Beauregard Lee and his network of groundhogs play a tactical part. While you are leader of all the Ground Forces, General Beauregard is leader of the Underground Movement. Through his efforts, skunks everywhere will be on the alert. After you win the Battle of Newton Hill, you'll be dispatched by Beauregard to other potential battle sites to organize new Skunk Troops."

"Sir, that sounds good in theory, but I can't be in more than one place at a time."

"True, Sebastian. As Commander in Chief, you will explain the Strategic Plan to a group of skunks and assign a leader who will conduct another confrontation. After each battleground is secured, the new leaders will be dispatched to continue the process. And thus the Skunk Army will spread. It's not just a single battle. It's all-out warfare, and we'll win against this enemy if we work together and follow our plan."

While Sebastian was being schooled in strategic planning, the First Skunk Troop was given a crash course by Coach Politella in all five chapters of *The Skunk's Art of Defense*. Politella spent the most time explaining the final chapter, the Strategic Plan, and how important it was for the First Skunk Troop to act as a single unit, obeying the Commander in Chief.

By the end of their respective training sessions it was dawn. The time had come for food, followed by rest, followed by farewells, followed by dusk, and then, finally, followed by departure. In the end, refreshed and recharged, Sebastian and his troops exited Enlightenment School to begin their passage back to the Newton property.

~ 22 ~

The Return

Although the return trip through Tunnel B held its own set of challenges, the skunks arrived safely after several suns and moons. Throughout their journey, Sebastian's ability to independently make decisions gave him the confidence to emerge as the unquestionable leader. When the long line of one hundred skunks, linked paw to tail, finally neared the junction of Tunnel B and the burrow, Sebastian saw a large animal off in the distance.

Beauregard, his large presence like a lighthouse, hailed them with paws held high. Overjoyed to see his friend and mentor, Sebastian rushed forward, followed by the First Skunk Troop. The skunks surrounded Beauregard and began to cheer.

The hubbub continued until Sebastian raised his voice above the din and commanded, "Atten...tion! General Beauregard has something to say."

"Well, well, well, mah old friends have arrived. I do declare, greeting y'all makes me so happy. But we got some bidness to tend to after y'all are nourished and refreshed. So follow me to the burruh's main room. Miss Abbey will bring something to eat the minute I let her know you're home."

Sebastian became animated at the mention of Abigail. "Let's hurry up. I can't wait to see Abbey and DJ. How about I tell Abbey we're back?"

Beauregard cleared his throat and, taking Sebastian aside, whispered, "Sebastian, first I need to talk to ya in private. Please excuse the First Skunk Troop and direct them to the main room."

With that Sebastian straightened up and said, "First Skunk Troop, Dismissed! Please depart for the main room. Beauregard and I have some matters to review."

After the skunks departed, Beauregard put his paw around Sebastian, drawing him close. "Now, I must warn ya, Sebastian. Miss Abbey is outta sorts. I'm hoping that seeing y'all again gives her some relief."

Sebastian questioned, "Why? What's the matter? Did something happen while we were gone? Relief from what?"

In a constrained and hesitant voice Beauregard continued. "Well, Sebastian, there are some things that happened while ya were gone that have caused Miss Abbey much consternation, and she's all up-set.'"

"Beauregard. Just say what it is. I need to know, even if it's hard."

Beauregard, taking a deep breath, but still not answering directly, said, "I also have two mighty good news reports and only one bad news report even though it's real bad."

Sebastian wiped his brow. "Okay, I'm ready to hear all of it, the bad and the good."

"Right. I'll start with the bad and finish up with the good since two good reports will cheer ya up after hearing the bad news. So here it goes. Ya remember how sick DJ was when you left?"

Sebastian answered, "Yes ..."

"Sebastian, I am so sorry to tell ya, DJ has done passed."

Sebastian did not understand. "What's that mean, passed?"

"I mean passed away ... died. DJ died not long after y'all left for Enlightenment."

Beauregard's words were like a smack across Sebastian's face and he winced, lurching backwards. "Oh, no! I knew he was getting worse. Why did I leave? I should have stayed with him until the end. It's probably my fault. If I had stayed he might still be alive."

"I know how ya feel but ya did the right thing. Ya had to go. Abbey's counting on ya to help save the land."

Beauregard allowed Sebastian a few minutes to weep before reminding Sebastian, "Don't forgit, I also have good news, some very good news indeed. Fact is, I have two things ta tell ya that will definitely make ya feel better, even better than better, if I may say so mahself. Are ya ready?"

"Beauregard, please, I can't imagine anything that'll make me feel better right now. I still haven't gotten over losing Willie, and now you tell me about DJ. It's more than I can bear."

"That's just it, Sebastian. One of the things I gotta tell ya is that Willie ...well, Willie was lost, but not gone."

"Not gone? You mean Willie survived the explosion at Hell's Bells?"

"That's exactly what I'm saying. Willie's alive."

"But how? When I surfaced from the underground, Hell's Bells was nothing but black billowing smoke and red-hot fire. It was a charred wasteland, and Willie was nowhere in sight. This is amazing! Where is he? I want to see him right away."

"Now Sebastian, ya gotta calm down and take it one step at a time. Willie's with Abbey. He needed a heap of caring for. I know you're excited, but first we gotta git ya some food and water. And I almost forgot, there is some more good news—"

But Sebastian didn't give Beauregard a chance to tell him about Sabrina. He had already rushed off in the direction of the burrow's main room where he hurriedly saluted the First Skunk Troop, passing them by on his way to the burrow's main exit.

As if shot out of a circus cannon, Sebastian flew out of the burrow and dashed to Abigail's house, intent on finding Willie. Within minutes Sebastian was scratching at Abigail's back door. It was a scratch that could only have been made by Sebastian and one that Abigail immediately recognized. She opened the door and Sebastian jumped into the house, scrambling up into Abigail's arms.

"Oh Sebastian, thank the Lord you're back." Abigail put Sebastian down. "Let me look at you. Wonderful! You're even healthier than before you left. And your second stripe is almost up to your head. Wow!"

Although Sebastian was thrilled to see Abbey, at that moment, it was Willie who was uppermost in his mind. "Abbey, Beauregard told me Willie didn't die and that you've been taking care of him. Where is he? Can I see him? Can I see him now?"

"Yes, but he was severely wounded. Perhaps seeing you will give him the strength he needs to finally heal. He's in ... in ...D—"

Before Abigail could say, DJ's room, she choked up. It wasn't until then that Sebastian noticed how gaunt Abigail looked, how dull her skin appeared, and how her bloodshot eyes were sunken into their sockets. She was the picture of self-neglect, and obviously heartbroken.

"Oh, Abbey, Beauregard told me about DJ. I am so sorry. I know how much you loved him, and so did I."

Abigail understood the attachment between Sebastian and DJ. She was thoughtful before responding. "You know, Sebastian, I think maybe our shared sadness will help us both recover."

"You're right, Abbey. And our fight against a common enemy will give you new purpose."

Sniffling, Abigail drew a tissue from her apron pocket and blew her nose. She peered into Sebastian's eyes and gathered him up into her arms and began petting his soft fur for comfort, hers and his.

"Let's go into DJ's room. It's where I've been tending Willie. And, oh, I almost forgot. There's another animal in there, too."

"Another animal?"

"Yes, a skunk, or should I say skunkette. Her name is Sabrina."

"Did I ever meet her?"

"Sort of. She was the trapped skunkette you noticed when you came here with Sir and Coach Politella. She's the one you asked Willie to free first. Remember? She wasn't well enough to travel with you and the rest of the skunks."

Sebastian felt a wave of embarrassment, but managed to keep his composure. "Yes, how could I have forgotten? How is ... what is her name?"

"Sabrina. Her name is Sabrina. It means Legendary Princess."

"She's a princess?"

"Yup. Now brace yourself. I have something important to reveal. Sabrina is the Great[15] Granddaughter of Celeste."

"But that means she's related to Norton Bulymur, my Great[15] Grandfather."

"Correct. She's a distant relative of yours, and I can't wait until you meet her."

"Let's go, Abbey. But I really don't care about seeing Sabrina right now. I just need to see Willie."

"Okay, but let me warn you. Willie was burned in the explosion and is still under wraps."

"Under wraps?"

Abigail answered, "Not only was Willie's fur smoldering when he arrived at my door, but the hide underneath his singed fur was badly burned. I took him to the animal hospital right away. Dr. Murphy removed as much fur as possible and then covered Willie's hide with a bandage coated in a special aloe ointment. I change the bandages every few days. That's what I meant when I said Willie's still under wraps."

Sebastian was concerned but hopeful. "I don't care how Willie looks, only how he feels. Is he in pain?"

"The pain is subsiding, what with the aloe treatments and the pain medication which also helps. But it makes him a little woozy. So even though he's most anxious to see you again, he won't be the same exuberant Willie you're used to."

"That's okay. Abbey, thanks for explaining. I understand and I'm ready to see him no matter what."

Abigail released Sebastian from her arms, placing him on the floor. The two left the kitchen and headed for the one-time sickroom which had been DJ's.

"Sebastian, wait at the door so I can prepare Willie. I don't want to shock or overexcite him. But first, let me get some fresh air in here"

Abigail opened the window, allowing a frosty breeze to enter and cleanse the previous sickroom. Then she walked over to Willie, who was curled up resting in DJ's old hospital bed. He was encased in bandages wrapped around his entire body, head, and tail. The only visible indications that identified Willie as Willie were his nose, mouth, and eyes. Willie glanced beseechingly up at Abigail, telegraphing his need for pain medication.

Using a slow and tender voice, Abigail said, "Willie, before I give you your medicine, there's someone here who wants to see you."

Tight-lipped, Willie asked, "Who's here, Abbey?"

"I don't want you to get too excited. Take a deep breath and blow it out slowly through your nose. Willie, Sebastian is here. Look over by the doorway."

Willie's eyes grew misty as he gazed at his beloved cousin. He gasped and then, in a constrained voice, said, "Sebastian. Oh, Sebastian."

From the doorway, Sebastian slowly approached. Once at Willie's bedside, he jumped into the familiar bed where he had spent so many hours comforting DJ. Now it was time to comfort Willie. Grateful to have his cousin and longtime friend back, Sebastian curled up next to Willie. Neither spoke. No words were necessary. All was understood.

Sebastian didn't register the presence of Sabrina, snuggled in a soft throw lying across an armchair in the corner of the room, until Abigail beckoned her to come along, leaving Willie and Sebastian to themselves. As Sabrina stretched out before vacating the chair, her elongated body with its thick shiny fur and two neon white stripes did not escape Sebastian's notice. Lifting his head ever so slightly to view Sabrina and inhale her delightful musky scent, Sebastian caught her demurely glancing at him. Both quickly looked away. It was only a moment, but it was the moment in which each knew they would become life-mates.

That evening Sebastian left, returning to his troops in the backyard burrow. He was inspired with the knowledge that Willie was safe, Sabrina would be his lifelong partner, and Abigail, although still sad, would move on with a new purpose. Together they would make a difference in their shared world.

230

~ 23 ~

The Snow Moon

Time seemed to inch along for all the waiting players —Willie, waiting for his fur to grow back, Sebastian and the Skunk Troop waiting for battle, Abigail waiting to secure her land, Beauregard waiting to alert distant groundhogs, and the enemy waiting to make the first move. The Wolf Moon had come and gone.

Sebastian and the First Troop had been holding out underground for several weeks, waiting for the inevitable. Beauregard had departed for parts unknown, but promised to catch up with them at some point. Abbey continued to bring food and water. From time to time Sebastian left the burrow to check on Willie's progress. It took two weeks before Willie's bandages could be removed. At first even the feel of air on his body caused him to wince with pain.

With each departure and return, Sebastian knew he was taking a chance but was compelled to be certain that Willie was improving. Moreover, Sebastian needed time to court Sabrina. So his comings and goings were made with trepidation—and fortunately without incident. By the third week, Sebastian had won Sabrina's heart, and the two were to be mated after the first skirmish, which couldn't come soon enough for either. It was the first night of the Snow Moon and all was readied. Each player knew his part. The only unknown, which is always unknown to all players in all tales everywhere, was the ending.

Abigail, Willie, and Sabrina were gathered in the kitchen, peering through the patio's glass door. The night was clear and cold, with new snow sparkling like diamonds. The stars twinkled extra brightly as if polished with silver cream, and the moon was a perfect round ball of glittering light illuminating the back yard and woodlands.

Abigail was distracted by what she noted as fuzz growing on Willie. "Wow, Willie, now that your bandages have been removed, I can see your fur is starting to grow back."

Willie asked, "Is it still white?"

"Yup. White as the new snow falling outside."

Willie, adjusting his eyes, peered at the figure reflected in the glass of the patio door. That's when he saw himself and breathed a deep sigh of relief followed by an exuberant laugh.

"Oh, Abbey, how can I ever thank you for all you've done, for me and for Sebastian, too?"

Sabrina chimed in, "And don't forget about me. Abbey you're a wonder. You've helped all of us through very difficult times. You've been our healer."

Abigail said, "Thank you both, but you helped me as much as I helped you."

The three friends were watching the snow blanket the Earth and gild the trees when their private reveries were interrupted by something in the distance, coming from the direction of the woods. To Abigail it sounded like a low rumble. Willie and Sabrina, who could feel the vibrations from which the sound came, also heard a rumble, but magnified many times over by their keen sense of hearing. All three listened to the muted sound as it moved slowly up Newton Hill along a new road recently carved in the woodlands.

Willie began to shake. "It's them! It's the monsters—I mean the machines. They're coming! And they'll be here in a few minutes. Hurry, Abbey, you need to warn Sebastian and the First Skunk Troop."

"Willie, are you sure?" Abigail asked.

"Absolutely! It's the same sound I heard when I was a kit. The monster machines will be here to clear the land, only this time it won't be for homes. It'll be for drilling. Abbey, you never even signed the lease."

"I know. But they're coming anyway."

Sabrina, who hadn't said anything yet, voiced her opinion. "Just like you read in the newspaper the other day, Abbey. They'll do it because they can, and so far no one seems to be able to stop them. But now there's a plan, and it will work."

Abigail asked Sabrina, "How do you know it'll work?"

"I know, because Together We Can," Sabrina answered in a self-assured voice. She said *Together We Can* with such emphasis that all three began to chant loudly.

"Together We Can! Together We Can! Together We Can!"

Abigail grabbed her coat and donned her boots, saying, "I'm going to warn Sebastian!" In her haste, she forgot hat, scarf, and gloves.

She stepped into the snow pile in front of the door and almost slipped, but caught herself just as the wind picked up, turning the gentle snowfall into a squall. The snow swirled as if whipped by a magical hand, making progress difficult. When she finally arrived at the burrow, Abigail bent down and scraped away the snow that covered the opening. She yelled above the howling wind, "Sebastian, it's time. Get ready! Can you hear me?"

The animals had become restless, and it was with great relief that Sebastian and the rest of the skunks felt the vibrations of oncoming machines and heard Abigail's shouted warning.

Abigail waited for a response from Sebastian and was relieved when she heard muffled orders being given.

"Atten...tion! First Troop, the enemy is approaching. Line up, tail to tail. Ready, march. One. Two. Three. Four."

Despite the cold, Abigail watched Sebastian and the First Skunk Troop march out of the burrow and off into the night. It wasn't until the one hundredth skunk's tail could no longer be seen that Abigail returned to Willie and Sabrina, who were anxiously awaiting news. Not wanting to display her own state of apprehension, Abigail calmly said, "Well, they're on their way. All we can do now is pray."

* * *

Following the Strategic Plan, Sebastian and his First Skunk Troop marched along the cleared path to the designated point at the edge of the woodlands. After arriving, they lined up single file, facing the sound of the advancing enemy. The snow was still coming down heavily and quickly covered them, creating the perfect camouflage. Nevertheless, they remained warm and cozy, protected by their natural thick fur. The First Skunk Troop was well hidden, and ready to challenge an unsuspecting enemy. Despite the might of the malevolent machines, the skunks had one main advantage, the element of surprise.

While undercover, Sebastian and the First Skunk Troop kept their ears to the frosty ground, listening for the arrival of the diggers, haulers, and tankers. The crunch and rumble of the machines could be felt and heard by the awaiting soldiers. The closer the machines got, the greater the vibrations and the louder the rumble. It sounded like thunder, making their small bones quiver.

Once the machines arrived and the motors were turned off, all was still. That's when Sebastian surfaced just above the snow and began to hiss, setting the tone loudly enough for the troops to hear.

Raising his voice, he commanded, "First Skunk Troop! Ready! Commence hissing!"

The First Skunk Troop, heads just above the snow, began a clamor of raspy squeaks and squeals. It sounded like the string instruments of an orchestra tuning up in high staccato notes. They continued making this racket until Sebastian's next command.

"First Skunk Troop! Halt hissing! Take cover!" Quickly the troop ducked down into the snow so they wouldn't be seen. When there was no response from the enemy, Sebastian surfaced again.

"First Skunk Troop! Commence vocal threat with increased volume!"

Again the skunks surfaced just above the snow, making their vocal threats louder and then ducked down again.

From about one hundred feet away, Sebastian could hear the mumble of men. Without completely revealing himself, he lifted his head to peer out from under the snow. What Sebastian saw was a gang of truck drivers and workmen, all wearing woolen caps underneath hardhats, gloves and bulky jackets, who had stepped out from their convoy of enormous trucks. They were facing Sebastian and his army of skunks. What Sebastian heard was the slamming of truck doors and loud voices.

"What the heck was that?"

"Don't know, boss. Sounded weird, like a bunch of squeaks."

Then a different voice yelled, "Yeah, like some kind of animals. I don't see 'em anywhere."

"Joe, you see anything on your end?" the boss hollered.

"Nope. Don't see nothing. But sure sounds like whatever it is ... is right in front of us, stretching out from left to right. Whadya wanna do about it?"

"Get back in your trucks and start blowin' them horns. It'll scare off whatever it is," the boss ordered.

"You got it, boss!"

The men got in their trucks, slamming the doors behind them, and began honking their horns. Although it was the enemy's attempt to scare off whatever was in front of them, to the army of skunks, it was a moment of truth or dare.

What ensued next was a volley of audible exchanges between the animals and the machines. Each time the skunk army would hiss, the truck horns would blare. As the hissing got louder and shriller, the honks became more rapid in succession and longer in duration.

The exchange was like the escalation of an argument during the process of negotiating a deal, the deal in this case being the withdrawal of the trucks versus forcing whatever was out there to vamoose. This went on until both the hissing and the honking were simultaneous, waking the surrounding neighbors who stood at their windows watching the mysterious confrontation unfold. Despite the presence of only ten trucks to one hundred and one skunks, the honks and blares were far more forceful, drowning out the squeaks of the skunks.

Sebastian raised his voice over the blasts yelling out his next command. "First Skunk Troop! Ready! Reveal!"

With that all the skunks emerged and shook the snow from their backs and heads.

Before the workers had a chance to grab weapons of any kind, whether guns in their trucks or explosives to clear the land, Sebastian gave his next command.

"First Skunk Troop! Ready! Commence thump roll!"

The men heard a crescendo of thumping sounds like a drum roll emanating from the longest line of small black animals they had ever seen. Fortunately for the skunks, swirling snow made it difficult for the men to discern the distinctive white stripes. The headlight beams further intensified the visual distortion.

"Cut your lights," the crew boss shouted. But even without the headlights, the bright light of the Snow Moon cast a glare that continued to camouflage the skunks.

When the thumping became ominously faster and louder, the workers again climbed out of their trucks and the boss asked, "Any of you ever seen or heard anything like this before?"

An answer came from the driver in the middle of the truck caravan. "Yup! But not from so many of 'em at once."

"So many of what? What in blazes are they?"

"Well, boss, I hate to tell you, but it's a bunch— and I mean a big bunch— of skunks... maybe even a thousand of 'em."

"Skunks? For crying out loud! What are they doing here? I thought that fella Higbee from that exterminating company rounded 'em up and got rid of 'em."

"Nah. Didn't you read that newspaper article last month about how a whole lot of 'em escaped after someone tripped the traps?"

"Yeah, I do remember something 'bout that. But that don't explain this!"

Another driver spoke up. "If it's skunks, then the next thing they're gonna do is shoot their skunk spray at us."

The crew boss looked at the driver. "But why would they do that?"

"Because they must think we're an enemy, that's why."

"Makes no sense to me. The only one out here that thinks we're the enemy is that crazy 'green' lady that won't sign the land lease. Her and a band of her buddies are causing all kinds of trouble. Environmental terrorists, if you ask me. That's what we're supposed to call 'em nowadays. They don't know what real green is! And I'm talking money. The land man done offered 'em all plenty, but they still refuse to sign. That's how come we had to sneak in here in the middle of the night. The big boss, Red, said just do it. So here we are."

Suddenly the thumping stopped and the night became quiet. The crew boss hollered, "Listen up! I don't hear no more thumping. Bet we scared 'em good."

Then the driver from the middle truck spoke up again. "Nope. That's just the calm before the storm. I'm tellin' ya, boss. Them skunks are gonna attack! It's the next step. So we better move outta here, the faster and farther the better."

"You've gotta be kidding me! Red will go crazy. I can't even imagine what he'll do."

Since neither their hissing nor their thumping seemed to have scared the men into leaving, Sebastian gave what he hoped would be his final commands. "First Skunk Troop! Ready! About face!"

The skunks turned their backs to the trucks and workmen. Sebastian followed with, "First Skunk Troop! Present tails!"

The skunks did as they were commanded and lifted their tails. After a moment they could hear the collective screams of the workers behind them who were finally realizing what was about to happen. The abrupt slamming of truck doors was followed by rumbles and the movement of many vehicles as the enemy beat a hasty retreat.

~ 24 ~

A New Beginning

With the enemy routed, Sebastian again commanded, "First Skunk Troop! About face!"

The skunks turned around just in time to witness the enemy's retreat and raised a noisy cheer.

Sebastian held up his paw and waited until the roar subsided and said, "You did it! The plan worked! You won the first battle!"

Then a small voice, from the middle of the row of soldiers, asked, "May I speak, General Sebastian?"

"First Skunk Troop! At ease!" Sebastian commanded. "Of course, soldier. Please step out and speak up."

The soldier stepped out and raising his voice said, "Two things, sir. First of all, we did it! We won the battle and never could have done it without your great leadership. Second, what did you mean by winning our first battle? Will there be others to come?"

"Most assuredly," Sebastian answered. "This campaign is greater than one battle. It's a war, and we'll need to confront the enemy wherever and whenever he attacks."

Then another soldier asked, "How will we know when to reconvene?"

Sebastian explained the details. "The underground network of groundhogs, organized by General Beauregard, will communicate when and where you or other troops are needed. All soldiers are to follow the Strategic Plan unless otherwise instructed."

"Other troops?"

"Yes, you are but the first of many."

"How many?"

"As many as it takes," Sebastian said. "Beauregard and the Groundhog Underground will organize skunk soldiers into troops everywhere they're needed. But now, it's time to return to our homes."

Sebastian drew himself up to his full height. "First Skunk Troop! Dismissed!"

With that, the skunk soldiers scattered, returning to their pursuit of enlightenment, whether informally from life experience or formally from their kit coaches at school. Only Sebastian remained, perplexed by a mixture of conflicting emotions. At first he was elated over what the soldiers had accomplished under his leadership. Shortly thereafter he felt a sense of loneliness and isolation, having severed the close ties established with his army of skunks. Ultimately, he felt a sense of unease, certain there would be more battles to come.

With the snow squalls having subsided, the bright Snow Moon lit the Newton's back yard, beckoning Sebastian to move forward by going back—back to Abigail, Willie, and Sabrina. Promises had been made and obligations needed to be honored.

The windswept snow created a sparkly drift on one side of the yard and a slippery path on the other. Sebastian was halfway to Abigail's house when his thoughts were interrupted by a strange sensation intensifying with each step. At first it was an itch on the left side of his back. Then it became a twitch, morphing into a prickle. Finally, Sebastian felt the tingle of small electric shocks coursing up and down from the nape of his neck, up over his head, and down to his nose. Unlike the feeling of cold wetness followed by pain and fear when he was de-tailed by the road striper so long ago, this sensation was both pleasurable and exciting.

* * *

Abigail, Willie, and Sabrina had been peering out the kitchen's patio door for what seemed an eternity. They couldn't see what had happened in the distance, but they could hear the rumble and grind of motors. As the swirling snow subsided, Abigail could see Sebastian coming toward the house. She slid open the glass patio door. Joined by Willie and Sabrina, the three began to rejoice with whoops, hollers, and bravos, even before Sebastian arrived. Once Sebastian entered the house, all four gathered in a group hug.

It was Willie who first noted Sebastian's head and shoulder. He let out a shrill squeal. "Oh, my stars! Oh, for the love of our Great[15] Grandfathers and Grandmothers! It's happened! The curse of the stripeless skunk has been lifted. Sebastian, I told you so. You were the one chosen to lift the curse. And you did it. You did it! You earned both your stripes!"

Everyone was transfixed by the sight of Sebastian's two completed white stripes. Not only did the stripes glow with a beautiful luminescence, but they seemed to pulse with mysterious warmth, almost as if alive.

Sebastian was ecstatic. He didn't need to see the stripes, because he could feel them running down his back, joining at the top of his head and continuing in a single stripe down his nose. He knew they were real and knew they were permanent. Eventually the pulsing stopped, but the bright white stripes remained as a beacon, lighting the way for others to choose the preservation of Earth and her inhabitants over the false gods of greed and power.

* * *

And so it was that the four friends stood just inside the door, each projecting love, appreciation, and gratitude to the others for all that had transpired among them. They knew their life paths had merged for a time, while traveling to the same destination. And they knew that even though this was "so long" rather than "goodbye," their memories would sustain and strengthen them until they would meet again.

Sebastian, Sabrina, and Willie scurried into the woods. They could see Abigail still standing in the doorway when they stopped for an instant, looking back in the direction where they had found warmth and healing, purpose and love.

A gust of wind swirled a dusting of snow around Abigail's feet. As they watched, Abigail turned toward the kitchen, opening the door against the wind. Before the door closed, faint strains from the radio reached the animals. One of Abigail's favorite tunes was playing. It seemed almost prophetic to hear Dylan singing, "The answer, my friend, is blowin' in the wind. The answer is blowin' in the wind."

About Dylan Weiss

Dylan, a speech-language pathologist for more than thirty-five years, specialized in geriatric communication disorders and progressive neurologic disease. When her mother developed Parkinson's and could not get treatment due to misunderstood Medicare regulations, she was inspired to make a difference by writing "Reimbursable Geriatric Service Delivery, a Functional Maintenance Therapy System" which became a bestseller in her profession.

After her husband was diagnosed with Alzheimer's disease, Dylan retired from a successful career and became a caregiver for the next fifteen years. Again, she was inspired to write, documenting the challenges they faced and the creative communication programs she developed throughout his decline. Dylan's article, "Sharing the Load," won an Excel Award from the Society of National Association of Publishers in the literary category.

Dylan became a community leader, sitting on Parks and Recreation boards, improving the township's parks system, promoting green efforts, and all the while, expanding her writing efforts with an intent on exposing a potential environmental predator—unconventional natural gas hydraulic fracking.

Dylan's hope is that readers of Sebastian's Tale are inspired to make a difference.

Visit Dylan on the web at: www.SebastiansTale.com.

CPSIA information can be obtained
at www.ICGtesting.com
Printed in the USA
FFOW01n0216160916
27675FF